NORTH

HUNTER SQUAD
BOOK 2

ANNA HACKETT

North

Published by Anna Hackett

Copyright 2025 by Anna Hackett

Cover by Hang Le Designs

Cover image by Wander Aguiar

Edits by Tanya Saari

ISBN (ebook): 978-1-923134-61-4

ISBN (paperback): 978-1-923134-62-1

This book is a work of fiction. All names, characters, places and incidents are either the product of the author's imagination or are used fictitiously. Any resemblance to actual persons, events or places is coincidental. No part of this book may be reproduced, scanned, or distributed in any printed or electronic form.

WHAT READERS ARE SAYING ABOUT ANNA'S ACTION ROMANCE

The Powerbroker - Romantic Book of the Year (Ruby) winner 2022

Heart of Eon - Romantic Book of the Year (Ruby) winner 2020

Cyborg - PRISM Award Winner 2019

Unfathomed and Unmapped - Romantic Book of the Year (Ruby) finalists 2018

Unexplored – Romantic Book of the Year (Ruby) Novella Winner 2017

Return to Dark Earth – One of Library Journal's Best E-Original Books for 2015 and two-time SFR Galaxy Awards winner

At Star's End – One of Library Journal's Best E-Original Romances for 2014

The Phoenix Adventures – SFR Galaxy Award Winner for Most Fun New Series and "Why Isn't This a Movie?" Series

Beneath a Trojan Moon – SFR Galaxy Award Winner and RWAus Ella Award Winner

Hell Squad – SFR Galaxy Award for best Post-Apocalypse for Readers who don't like Post-Apocalypse

"Like Indiana Jones meets Star Wars. A treasure hunt with a steamy romance." – SFF Dragon, review of *Among Galactic Ruins*

"Action, danger, aliens, romance – yup, it's another great book from Anna Hackett!" – Book Gannet Reviews, review of *Hell Squad: Marcus*

Sign up for my VIP mailing list and get your *free box set* containing three action-packed romances.

Visit here to get started: www.annahackett.com

CHAPTER ONE

HUNTER SQUAD

Jess

I kept my face pressed to the quadcopter window, looking out at the long stretch of golden beach below.

I'd lived in Australia for three weeks now, and I loved it. To be fair, I hadn't seen much of my new home since I'd been too busy working. But what I had seen, I liked. The weather was fantastic, the house I'd been given was cute and comfortable, and the landscape was amazing—from rolling green hills to swathes of native bushland. It was so different to where I'd grown up in Southern California.

Below, I watched the waves crashing onto the sand, mesmerized by the stunning shade of blue. The beaches did remind me of home. It was hard to imagine what it must have been like when our parents were kids, when they were able to swim and play at the beach. I'd heard stories of picnics on the sand, beach volleyball, and every inch of sand covered in towels, umbrellas, and sunbathing bodies.

Not anymore.

Ahead, we approached the remnants of a ruined seaside town. I leaned forward. The buildings were all destroyed to varying degrees, vegetation reclaiming the land and growing out through doors and windows. Several overturned, rusted cars littered the streets. My mouth tightened.

Not all parts were so beautiful.

Thirty years ago, an alien invasion had decimated not only Australia, but the entire planet.

Humans had fought back and won. The Gizzida—reptilian, dinosaur-like aliens—had been defeated. But they'd left a planet-wide trail of destruction in their wake.

"I have a visual," a female voice said from the cockpit. "Two minutes to contact with the creatures."

I straightened, my hands gripping my carbine weapon.

The aliens had also left behind horrible, dangerous hybrid creatures. In their labs, they'd mixed their DNA with that of Earth's native fauna. They'd created monsters that liked to hunt...and were hungry.

I glanced across the quadcopter, my gaze taking in the tough soldiers sitting beside me. I'd moved all the way to Australia to join Hunter Squad. They were known all over the world as one of the top monster-hunting squads on the planet. I'd done similar work with the military in the United States, alongside my science studies. My focus had revolved around researching the monsters.

No two creatures were alike. They'd mutated and

bred, and held little resemblance to the animals used to create them. Every time I thought I'd found an answer on how to eradicate them, I discovered a dozen more questions.

I looked at Jameson Steele, seated across from me. He was our squad leader, and the son of Marcus Steele, legendary leader of the famed Hell Squad. Hell Squad had been instrumental in beating the Gizzida.

Marcus' son took after him. Jameson had rugged features and was a hell of a leader—strong, steady, and good with a carbine.

He caught my gaze and gave me a chin lift.

I nodded. *Yes, I was ready.*

Next to Jameson, sat Kai Rahia. Tall, leaner, with black hair and brown skin, he was the squad's second-in-command, and an excellent tracker.

Then there were the twins—Zeke and Marc Jackson. They looked near identical with muscular bodies and tanned skin, except Zeke kept his dark hair cut short and Marc's was longer and shaggy. Other than that, they were total opposites. Night and day. Zeke was quiet, and Marc talked, laughed, and joked all the time.

The last soldier on the team was our medic—North Connors.

I controlled my scowl. He hadn't been unfriendly, but he hadn't exactly been welcoming, either. It was like he'd taken one look at me, and put me on probation. I looked at him through my lashes. The man had a hell of a face—a cut jaw, handsome features. I'd seen more than more one woman flutter her lashes at him over the last few weeks.

I was used to proving myself. When I'd first joined the squads back home, I'd had to work with people who either underestimated me or felt the need to protect me. There'd been one idiot who'd leaped in front of me every time we were in a fight. I'd had to disabuse him of that instinct. I'd been raised by a single dad, and he'd taught me to stand on my own two feet. He'd always told me to never let any obstacle get in my way. My heart squeezed. I missed him. He'd died a year ago, but some days, it felt like yesterday. We'd lost my mom when I'd been a toddler. She'd been injured in the invasion, and had battled ongoing health issues in the years after.

But we had a big extended family, and dad had made sure I'd never felt the lack.

But losing dad...

It's why I'd left San Diego and moved to Australia. I shifted on my seat. Everything back home reminded me of him. I'd had to get away.

When my Uncle Cruz—although technically he was just a distant cousin—had told me that Hunter Squad needed a new member, I'd leaped at the chance.

Jameson had been welcoming, as had the others, but North did not seem happy.

His gaze met mine across the Talon quadcopter. He had ice-blue eyes surrounded by a ring of dark blue.

I lifted my chin. No one intimidated me. I didn't know what his problem was, but I had the skills and experience to be here.

We had a little stare-off until our pilot spoke again.

"I've seen some ugly monsters before, but these ones might win the prize," Colbie said.

I wasn't the lone female on the squad. Our pilot was the best quadcopter pilot I'd ever flown with. Our comms officer—who was currently sitting back at base in the control room—was female, too. Sasha Rahia was Kai's cousin. They were both the children of other famous soldiers from the invasion.

All the people on this squad were the sons and daughters of legends. It was a privilege to be here.

Jameson rose and moved toward the cockpit. He grunted. "Ugly fuckers."

"All right, Hunter Squad—" Sasha's voice came through my earpiece clearly "—you're approaching the inhabited town of Swanhaven. The town guards spotted a small pack of monsters outside the walls today. They called us in."

I looked out the side window of the Talon. Six dark creatures were running up the beach. They looked misshapen, their gait off, but they were still fast. They reminded me of dogs...sort of.

I wished I had time to snap some images and take some notes. I had a huge database of monster types and characteristics.

Later, Jess. For now, stop the nasty monsters, then you can study them.

"Hunter Squad," Jameson said. "Let's do our thing."

Marc tapped his carbine. "Let's put down some monsters."

I glanced at North one more time and found his cool gaze on me. Then I looked away and gripped my carbine as the Talon lowered toward the beach.

I had monsters to kill.

North

I DOUBLE CHECKED my medical backpack.

When we were in the field, if someone was injured—I was it. Next, I checked my weapons. My carbine was fully charged, and my combat knife was in place in the sheath on my thigh. I tapped my fist against the armor plating on my chest. We all wore lightweight, protective armor.

Time to go monster hunting.

Jameson slid the side door of the Talon open. I watched Jessica Ramos leap out. She was short and curvy, but all toned muscle. And she knew how to use her carbine.

You shouldn't be looking at her ass, Connors. She's your squad mate.

Gritting my teeth, I jumped out of the Talon. The sand shifted under my boots. Lifting my head, I spotted the monster pack ahead. They were making low, throaty noises.

"Form up," Jameson ordered.

We jogged up the beach in a tight group. Despite the warm, yellow sand, no one frolicked on the beach, or swam in the ocean anymore. I shot a quick glance at the waves. A second later, the shadow of a large, sharklike shape moved through the water. The Gizzida had left monsters in the ocean too. It was no longer safe to swim.

In New Sydney, at the famous Bondi Beach, they'd created a seawall to form an ocean pool. It was mostly safe to swim there, but the monsters still occasionally tried to climb or jump the wall.

I refocused on the monsters ahead of me. They turned and saw us coming. They made some weird, grunting noises.

They were ugly things. They moved on four legs, and had bulbous backs, with bumpy, brown, scaly skin. One of them skittered around, kicking up sand, and the skin on its back was almost translucent. Through it, I could see an ugly, greenish-yellow glow.

I frowned. I wasn't sure what it was, but I was certain that it wasn't good. "They have some sort of fluid in that back bulge. Be careful."

My squad all murmured their acknowledgment.

We'd learned the hard way that the monsters were often poisonous.

One of the pack, the largest creature, let out a grunt. As a group, they rushed toward us.

"Come to papa," Marc said.

We all aimed our carbines and fired.

The monsters shuddered under the laser fire, and several broke off, running for the nearby sand dunes. One got clear of the carbine fire and jumped at us.

Jess lunged forward, dropping to one knee, and fired up at it. The back of the monster burst, greenish-yellow goop hitting the sand. I tensed, but Jess rolled to the right and out of the line of fire. The creature's body hit the ground and twitched on the sand.

"Oh, gross," Marc said.

The sand sizzled. The stuff in its back was like acid.

"Follow the others," Jameson barked.

We turned right and ran toward the sand dunes. I heard two loud grunts, and two of the creatures rushed at us.

"No, you don't." Jess fired her carbine, jogging up the sand dune, focused and calm.

The creatures dodged, skittering backward.

"There's another one still on the beach," Zeke said. He diverted to attack it.

"I've got your six, bro." His brother followed him.

Ahead of me, Jess crested the small sand dune, then froze. "Oh, fuck. Back up!"

She ran back toward me, her boots skidding in the sand.

"Hunter Squad, I'm picking up a huge bunch of signatures ahead," Sasha said. "They appeared out of nowhere. Watch out!"

A swarm of the creatures came over the dune.

Fuck.

"They were hiding in the sand," Jess yelled.

We sprayed them with laser fire, and I heard Jameson curse. I ripped a grenade off my belt, touched the button, and tossed it.

Jess was almost back to me. I kept firing at the crest. The closest monster to her nipped at her heels. Weirdly, its body was shaking uncontrollably.

What was wrong with it?

"Hurry up, Jess." I aimed my carbine at it, just as it exploded.

Green-yellow goo flew everywhere.

I ducked. Some fluid splattered on the sand centimeters away. I watched the sand dissolve with a hiss.

Hell, Jess had been too close to it.

I lifted my head and saw her fall to the sand. She rolled down the dune. Jameson and Kai kept firing on the last of the pack.

Pushing up, I raced over to her.

She rolled over, her face panicked. "Shit, it burns."

The goop was eating into her armor on her back and side. I unbuckled the straps on her chest armor and ripped it off her. "You're okay. It'll be okay."

I saw her shirt had been burned through, and there was a nasty burn on her side and under her ribs. It extended around her back.

"*God.*" She hissed, biting her tongue.

"Hold on, Jess." I glanced up to make sure Jameson and Kai had us covered, then I tore my backpack open. I yanked out a pressure injector, dialed up the dosage and pressed it to her neck. It was a dose of painkiller and antibiotics.

"That'll help," I told her. "Hold still." I yanked out a tube of med gel and started spreading it generously over her burns. The enhanced gel accelerated healing.

Her tense body relaxed. I carefully treated the burns, trying not to notice her tanned skin. I half listened to the squad taking out the last of the monsters.

"Have you seen a monster like that before?" I asked her to distract her.

She ran a hand over her mouth. "No. Poisonous ones, yes. But not quite like these. None that exploded."

I dressed the burn, pressing adhesive bandages over it. I was careful not to hurt her. "Can't say I've seen them before, either."

She was quiet for a beat. "I think that's the most you've ever said to me." Her brow creased. "You're trying to distract me."

I met her dark gaze. "Is it working?"

"Yeah." She heaved out a breath.

"You'll need a dose of nano-meds when we get back to base. You'll be as good as new. Not even a scar."

She shrugged a shoulder. "I don't care about scars."

"It would be a shame to mar your pretty skin."

Her gaze flicked to mine. *Hell, why had I said that?*

My gaze dropped from her liquid brown eyes to the freckles sprinkled over her nose and cheeks.

Jessica Ramos messed with my brain. I ground my teeth together. That was the only explanation for why I was excruciatingly aware of her, why being near her made my damn skin itch. I didn't like it. I was steady, dependable. My job depended on that. Hell, people's lives depended on it. I didn't like when I felt out of control.

I hadn't been keen when I'd heard she was joining the squad. We hadn't had much luck with our last few recruits, and Jess was an outsider. She wasn't from around here. I was worried she'd upset the rhythm of the squad. I glanced over and saw Jameson slapping Kai on the shoulder. Several dead monsters lay at their feet.

The members of Hunter Squad were like family. We'd grown up together, and I'd do anything to keep them safe.

"Those things lured us into the dunes where more were waiting," Jess said quietly.

"Yeah." Lately the monsters were displaying

disturbing behaviors. Communicating with each other, working together. It was more than a little worrying.

"I've seen packs of similar monsters have a loose hierarchy." She stared at the dead creature. "And show some signs of cooperation, but not like this."

I finished pressing an adhesive bandage on her wound.

"Thanks, North." She touched the bandage.

I nodded.

Then Jess pulled out her comm unit, increased the screen size, and started taking notes.

"What are you doing?"

She didn't look up. "I want to note down everything on these monsters." Her fingers flew over the screen. "Description, behaviors." Her focus was on her device.

I watched her and realized she'd forgotten I was there.

Good. I straightened and packed up my backpack. Over the last few weeks, I'd seen that Jess was a good soldier. It looked like she was going to make it as a member of Hunter Squad.

She was my squad mate. That was it. Soon, I'd think of her just like the others.

And stop looking at her ass.

CHAPTER TWO

Jess

Warm fingers brushed over my side.

I pressed my lips together and focused on the comm screen. But of course, I didn't see anything, I only felt North's touch as he checked my bandage again. He had nice hands—strong, with well-shaped fingers.

I released a breath. *Get a grip, Jess. The man doesn't even like you.*

"How's the pain?" he asked.

"At about a two. The injection did its thing."

He nodded and rose. "Good."

He towered over me. My belly fluttered. *Stupid belly.* I stood as well and felt my side tug. I ruthlessly ignored it.

The man was built how I liked—tall, broad shoulders, lean hips, fit. I knew he had some tattoos because I had seen them on his arm in the squad locker room. He had thick, brown hair, with a few streaks of gold and a jaw that could cut steel.

He studied my damaged chest armor, frowning at the burned areas. "You can't put this back on."

"I'll be fine without it." I cocked my head. "I'm glad to see you have a decent bedside manner, especially when your general personality leans toward dislike and disapproval."

He frowned at me. "I don't dislike you."

I snorted. "Really? Ignoring me and glaring at me says otherwise."

He looked past me, toward the waves lapping the sand, and scraped a hand through his hair. "I don't hate you, Jess. I just don't trust you. These men—" he gestured to the squad in the distance "—are like brothers to me."

And I was the outsider.

"I just...don't want anything that will upset the balance of the squad," he added.

A part of me understood that. I couldn't argue with his need to protect his friends. I gave him a small nod. "I've got their back, North. And I've got yours, whether you believe it or not."

He was quiet for a beat. "And you'll always get the best medical treatment from me. I took an oath."

That's right. North wasn't just a medic, but a fully trained doctor. I wondered why he was on Hunter Squad and not working in a clinic or hospital somewhere.

"Hey." Jameson and the others jogged over. "Jess, are you all right?"

"I'm fine."

"She's got some burns from that substance in the monster. I treated her, but she'll need nano-meds when we get back to base."

Jameson nodded. "Okay, let's—"

"Jameson." Sasha's voice cut through the comm line.

Everyone straightened.

"I'm tracking a lone creature. It made it into the trees and is headed for the ruins of an abandoned town near your location."

Jameson cursed. "Okay, we're on it." He looked at us. "We can't let a monster with this acid stuff inside it stay on the loose around here." He eyed me. "I don't like that you don't have any chest armor."

"It's one creature." I lifted my chin. "I'll be fine, and I'll make sure I stay back."

North frowned. "That's against protocol."

I shot him a look. "From what I hear, you guys don't always follow protocol."

Marc smiled. "Protocol isn't that much fun."

I looked at Jameson. "If I stay here alone, I'm at higher risk of getting attacked by something than if I'm with you guys."

He stroked his stubbled jaw. "Okay, it is only one creature. Let's put it down and go home."

We trudged off the sand and into the trees. We moved onto an old road, where the pavement was cracked and weeds were growing through it. We made our way up the road, and came to some signs, rotting and falling down. One hung drunkenly from its post.

Welcome to Sussex Inlet.

As we walked into the derelict town, I wondered what had happened to the people who had lived here. There were thousands of places like this, once bustling with life, now turned into ghost towns.

The world had spent the last three decades rebuilding, but it took time. We'd lost skills and so many people. The population was slowly growing, and we were busy reconstructing so many skills and capabilities. Providing secure homes, power, and water had been the first items on the agenda for the burgeoning governments. Followed by education, food production, and medicine.

Prior to the invasion both the United States, Australia, and many other countries had been part of the United Coalition. After its collapse during the invasion, most governments were now small, and slowly starting to work together.

I knew we'd get there. Eventually. It was just going to take time. I scanned the ruins around me. We'd rebuild what we had before, but we'd do it even better. In ways that were better for the environment and people's health.

We approached a row of old shops. The glass fronts were smashed, and they'd probably been looted during the invasion. We turned a corner.

"Hell," Kai said. "Look at that."

It was a small Gizzida fighter ship. It had crashed into a store and the back end was pointing up through the broken roof.

"It's a ptero," Zeke said.

I'd seen pictures of the alien fighters. They had a distinctive pterosaur shape with large, fixed wings that sharpened to a pointed cockpit at the front, along with a long, tail-like back end.

We walked closer.

"Sash, any sign of the monster?" Jameson asked.

"Nothing yet."

I peered through the shattered window. "Oh wow. The Gizzida pilot is still in its seat."

The seat had listed sideways, with the mummified pilot still strapped to it. The gray, scaly skin now looked like leather. The alien's body was solid and muscular, and its face shrunken.

Marc peered over my shoulder. "He was a big fucker."

The humanoid Gizzida had been called raptors. They'd been the leadership and main foot soldiers of the Gizzida army. They'd been intelligent, cold, and cunning. I shivered.

"Split up in pairs," Jameson ordered. "Kai, you're with me. Zeke and Marc. North and Jess. Fan out and find the monster. My girlfriend is coming home today, and I want to get this done so we can get home before she gets back."

I knew that Jameson was dating an engineer, Greer Baird, who worked on a dam project nearby. She came home from the worksite every few days.

I met North's blue gaze. He jerked his head, and we headed down the empty street. Our boots echoed on the pavement. The town was eerie as hell.

North scanned around, alert. He might be a good doctor, but he was also a good soldier.

"Do you see it?" he asked.

"No."

I peered into a store. It looked like a clothes store, but most of the racks and hangers were empty.

"There!" North said.

Spinning, I looked up and saw the monster clamber

over a fallen brick wall into a larger store. The greenish-yellow glow from its back gave it away.

I touched my ear. "Sasha, we have a visual on the monster. North and I are in pursuit."

"Acknowledged," the comms officer replied.

"Don't let it get away," North clipped out.

We broke into a run and followed.

North

STEPPING INTO THE ABANDONED SHOP, I fought back the urge to sneeze. It had once been a grocery store and was filled with aisles of shelving. It looked dusty and forlorn, with old, desiccated leaves, and scraps of paper and rubbish on the floor.

Closer to Sydney, teams had started to dismantle the abandoned towns, and recycle what they found there. But farther out, towns like this one had sat untouched since the invasion. No doubt the people of Swanhaven had scavenged whatever they could from here.

As we walked inside, my boots crunched on twigs and rocks. The shelves were bare, and one set was tipped over. Toward the back of the store, the roof was caved in.

The monster was in here somewhere.

Jess moved forward, and I scowled at her. "You don't have any chest armor, so I'll take point."

She didn't look happy, but nodded.

There was a noise at the back, something falling. It hit the ground with a loud clatter. I whipped my carbine up and hurried down an aisle, Jess behind me. Another crashing noise and I swiveled.

Come on, asshole, stop hiding from us.

Then I saw a flash of movement at the end of the aisle, and swiveled my carbine and fired.

Whatever it was darted away in a flash. I cursed.

I pointed and we slowly continued on. We came to an area with old glass-fronted fridges, the doors hanging open. My boot crunched on some broken glass.

"Looks like people raided this during the invasion," she murmured.

"Yeah, my mom and dad said they had teams to scavenge for supplies to keep their base stocked. They'd search for food and medicines." Now we could create most of those things, but it had taken time to build capacity and abilities back up. The world was nothing like it had been before the invasion. Things were done in smaller batches, and on a priority basis. Smaller communities farther out depended on supply drops from New Sydney.

There was another noise, and I pointed. We moved into the next aisle.

My boots stuck to something on the floor, and I pulled a face. I lifted my foot. The sticky brown substance smelled bad. *Great.*

"North, there." Jess pointed quickly.

I looked up. The creature was perched on top of a shelf, like some weird gargoyle from the fairy tale stories my mom had read me as a kid.

We both fired at it, and it leaped off.

I was getting mad. I felt like it was playing with us.

NORTH

A loud, squawking noise broke the silence, and we quickly rounded the next aisle. Two birds took flight, and I caught a glimpse of colorful wings as they flew at us.

"Hell." Jess ducked and lifted an arm as they flew past her, and arrowed out the torn roof. She straightened. "They surprised me, but they were pretty."

"Rainbow lorikeets." Another flash of movement. "There's the monster."

It was scuttling across the floor at the back of the store, near the old deli section. I ran after it, circling some old counters that were covered in decades of dust. I fired.

The monster leaped onto a table, then over an old slicing machine. I fired again, and it jumped to the floor, and skittered back into the center of the store.

I growled and followed. It was *not* getting away.

I ran out near the aisles. "Do you see it?"

"No." Jess was walking slowly, scanning around.

I moved down an aisle quickly, straining to hear anything.

Creak.

"Watch out!" she shouted.

The shelves to my left started tilting. I turned, sprinting back toward the end of the aisle.

Jess waved at me. "Hurry."

I pushed for more speed, then jumped.

I landed flat on my front, just as the shelves crashed down behind me. They missed my boots by centimeters.

"That little fucker." I rose, dusting myself off.

"You okay?"

"I'm fine."

"North? Jess?" Sasha's voice. "Are you two all right?"

I touched my ear. "Yeah. We have the damn monster cornered in a store."

"Jameson and the others spotted something in the northeast quadrant. They're checking it out, then they'll head your way."

A skitter of sound at the back of the store had Jess swiveling, whipping her carbine up.

Then I heard something crashing at the front of the store.

"Are there two of them?" she said.

"Maybe something just fell." I looked at the front.

"I'll check out the back."

I frowned. "Jess, you don't have full armor."

"It's fine. I won't get close. Let's nail this thing and get out of here. It's creepy as hell."

I didn't like it, but I gave her a tight nod. "Be careful."

"I always am." She moved toward the back of the store, her ponytail swaying behind her.

Walking in the other direction, I came to a section of the store with smaller display cases. I took a few more steps, when something slammed into my knees.

Shit. The monster knocked me off my feet, making a squawking sound, its claws clicking on the tiles.

I rolled and got my carbine up.

The damn thing had been hiding under some shelves. I fired at it, and it jumped, its bulbous back glowing. It knocked into a display case and some leftover pairs of sunglasses tumbled onto the floor. The case crashed down and hit my legs.

Dammit, it was heavy. I was pinned to the floor. I

fired again. The creature was hopping around, and raced at me. It rammed into the carbine and sent the gun flying.

Fuck.

I tried to pull my legs free. I was trapped, dammit.

"Jess, I need—"

The creature leaped at me. I whipped my hands up, pressing my gloved palms to its torso. Its jaws snapped at me, and with a huge heave, I pushed it back. It did an ungraceful somersault on the floor, struggling to right itself.

"Come at me again," I growled. "I'll break your neck."

If the damn thing exploded on top of me, I'd be in a hell of a lot of trouble.

It snarled and launched at me again. *Fuck.* I threw my hands up.

Carbine fire erupted.

The creature made a gurgling noise and fell beside me with a thud.

Thank God. I sagged back. It had been a precision shot, which had missed the acidic goo on the creature's back.

I looked up at Jess.

She hurried forward, swung her carbine onto her shoulder, then gripped the shelves. She bent her legs and heaved. I helped as best I could. The shelves moved and I finally slid my legs out. Jess held out a hand.

After a second, I took it and let her pull me up.

We looked at each other.

"Thanks," I said.

"You're welcome." Her lips quirked. "I guess that makes us even now."

CHAPTER THREE

Jess

"Jess needs the infirmary, not me."

I hid a smile at North's grumble. We'd returned from the mission, but Jameson had been firm. I was going to the infirmary and so was North.

"You're getting checked out," Jameson said. "No arguing."

The men were walking behind me as we headed down the corridor. We were in the old underground base beneath Dawn—the Enclave. I'd read all about it in the reports on the alien invasion. It and Blue Mountain Base had been the main two bases the human survivors had utilized in the Sydney area.

The walls were concrete, and despite the artwork and really good natural lighting system, it still felt like a base. Ahead, I spotted the doors to the infirmary.

Trips to the doctor were never my favorite thing, but the burns on my side and back were stinging like hell.

Whatever painkillers North had given me were sadly wearing off.

"I'm not injured," North clipped out.

"Really?" Jameson snorted. "Despite fighting a monster and having heavy shelves tipped on top of you."

"Yes." A mutinous tone.

"Then why are you limping?"

North went quiet.

The doors to the infirmary whispered open. The walls were a soothing green and I saw medical staff in white coats bustling around. Several neat bunks lined one wall. A doctor and nurse were treating a young girl.

"What do we have here?" a female voice said.

I turned and saw a middle-aged, blonde woman headed our way. Her white coat flared around her body. Her hair was in a trim bob and she had a strong, attractive face.

"Your next victims, Doc," Jameson said.

"You bring me the best gifts, Jameson." She tilted her head, and Jameson pressed a kiss to her cheek. Then her blue gaze took me in before shifting to North. Her lips quirked. "This one makes the worst patient. All doctors and medics do."

"No, I don't," North muttered.

The doctor hugged him.

With a sigh, he hugged her back. "Hi, Aunt Emerson."

"Sit on the bunk. I'll make it as quick and as painless as possible."

"Treat Jess first." He sat on the edge of the bunk.

"She sustained significant burns to her left side and back." He rattled off the medications he'd given her.

Bright-blue eyes focused on her. "Hello, Jess, I'm Doctor Emerson Jackson-Green. Call me Doc Emerson."

"Jess Ramos." I realized this was Zeke and Marc's mother. She seemed much too small and elegant to have given birth to them.

"Jess is our newest squad member," Jameson said.

"So I've heard." Emerson cocked her head. "How are you holding up with this bunch of ruffians?"

"They're great." I flicked a quick glance at North. *Well, most of them.*

"I'll leave them in your capable hands. See you two at Hemi's." Jameson paused. "Once the doc clears you." He sent a hard look North's way, then left.

"Okay, Jess, let's see what you've done to yourself."

I laid back as the doctor tugged my shirt up. "North treated the burns in the field, I—"

"She needs nano-meds," North interjected. "The burns were caused by some acidic substance from a monster."

Emerson made a sympathetic noise, carefully peeling back the bandages North had applied.

"And he needs to get checked too." As the doc probed my side, I controlled a wince. "I'm pretty sure he's hurt his hip and cracked a rib."

"I'm *fine*."

Doc Emerson rolled her eyes. "My years of experience have led me to believe that it's in the male DNA to constantly say they're fine, even when they're not. My husband is the worst. That man can be bleeding all over the place and still tell me he's fine."

I smiled.

"Men," the doctor muttered.

"I can hear you," North said.

Doc Emerson winked. "I know." She probed my side again. "Oh, this does look nasty, although Dr. Connors there has done a good job. You will need nano-meds. It'll neutralize any other nasties that might have come from the monster."

I nodded.

"So you're Cruz's niece." Emerson pulled a trolley over, then lifted a vial.

"Sort of." I felt a tickle of nerves. Nano-meds squicked me out a little. "I think we're actually some sort of second cousin."

"Family is family. Now, lie back. I'll give you your dose of nano-meds, then check out Mr. 'I'm Fine'."

North made an annoyed sound.

I turned my head, and pale blue eyes caught mine. I blew out a breath. I reminded myself that nano-meds had come a long way from the days when they were just as likely to kill you rather than heal you.

From his seat on the bunk beside me, North frowned. "You haven't had nano-meds before?"

"Only once."

"There's no reason to be nervous. Doc Emerson is the best."

"It won't hurt a bit," the doctor said.

"I know." North kept staring at me. I huffed out a

breath. "I saw a squad mate have a bad reaction to them." I shuddered.

Emerson made a sympathetic sound. "It's rare but it happens. I promise we have everything we need to deal with an adverse reaction."

I didn't watch as she leaned over me to inject me. My stomach was full of uncomfortable flutters now.

"You'll be fine," North said.

I nodded.

He leaned forward and his fingers brushed mine. I let mine curl around his, and he gently squeezed.

I wasn't going to admit how comforting I found that small touch.

North

I SIPPED my beer and tried to relax.

Jess and I had been given a clean bill of health from Doc Emerson. My hip and ribs no longer ached. Best of all, Jess' burns were all healed. By the time Emerson was done, Jess didn't even have a hint of a scar.

We'd joined the squad at Hemi's bar, but for some reason, I couldn't relax. The place was busy and we'd snagged a prime table. Jess, Sasha, and Colbie sat at the end of the table, chatting up a storm.

"You all right?" Kai asked.

"Fine." I rolled my shoulders.

"You look like a man with woman problems," a voice said from across the table.

I looked up. Our dark-haired tech guru, Maxim Ivanov, cocked a brow at me. He was tall and lean, and kept his black hair long. Tonight it was tied back in a stubby ponytail.

"I don't have woman problems. There's no woman."

Maxim didn't look convinced. "Really?"

"Shouldn't you be in your workshop, grunting at everyone and inventing something?"

He sipped his vodka. "I needed a break."

Marc set some shot glasses down on the table. "A little celebration. To welcome the newest member of Hunter Squad."

Jess arched a brow. "You've bought me welcome drinks three times already, Jackson."

He grinned. "No? Really?"

"Any excuse with this one," Colbie said.

"Lark, that's not true."

"Lark?" Colbie's gaze narrowed.

"You didn't like sparrow, so I'm trying lark."

"Just quit with the nicknames."

Marc lifted a hand. "It's perfect for you. Larks are cute, sweet, and fly, just like you."

She rolled her eyes. If she did it any harder, they'd roll out of her head.

"Jess," Marc said. "These are thank-you drinks because you saved North's life."

Now, I frowned.

Jess glanced my way. "Technically he saved me first. On the beach."

Jameson snatched up a shot glass. "That's what good squad mates do. To Jess."

"To Jess," everyone echoed.

I took the shot glass and knocked it back, savoring the burn of Hemi's best whiskey.

Sasha smacked her lips. "Yum. This is the good stuff. Dad's special blend."

"Only the best for my girl," a deep voice said.

Sasha shot to her feet. "Dad!"

Hemi Rahia stepped into view. He was built like a tank. He wasn't the tallest in the bar, but his shoulders and chest were wide. His dark hair had a touch of a curl and was threaded with gray, and his smile was infectious.

He lifted Sasha off her feet and smacked a kiss to her lips. Hemi had three daughters. My dad always laughed about rough, tough, badass Hemi ending up as a girl dad.

But he adored his girls, including his wife, Cam.

Sasha took after her father—brown skin, curly, dark hair, and that big smile, but there was some of her mom in her, too, which showed in her high cheekbones and the line of her jaw.

"Are you working the bar today?" Sasha asked.

"I'm just checking in," Hemi rumbled. "Got to keep my employees on their toes. And you? Are you keeping your squad in one piece?"

"Always," she said.

"A good comms officer is worth their weight in pre-invasion whiskey." He pressed a kiss to Sasha's nose. "Hunter Squad, keep doing your thing."

I lifted my glass. "Always."

Hemi shook his head. "You look just like your dad."

Dad and Hemi were more than friends. They'd been berserkers on squad six together, led by Kai's dad, Tane.

"How are your parents?" Hemi asked.

"They're good. Enjoying their trip." Mom had been invited to do some work on computer systems redevelopment in Europe. She was in IT, and a tech guru. Dad had gone with her. "They'll be back in a month." Travel to other parts of the world took a lot longer than it had in the old days.

"Good, I miss them." Hemi's gaze shifted to Kai. "I think we need some better music in here."

Kai finished his drink. "Okay, Uncle Hemi."

The older man slapped Kai's shoulder. "Good man."

Kai walked over to the piano in the corner of the bar and sat on the stool. He sat there quietly for a minute, then pressed his hands to the keys and started to play.

It was some song I didn't recognize, but it sounded good. The bar quieted as everyone turned to listen. Soon, Kai was lost in the music and bent over the keys.

"Wow," Jess said.

"He's really good," I murmured.

"He's way beyond good."

"His mom wanted to learn to play. He took lessons with her. They're both really good."

Jess watched Kai for a bit. "His mom's an alien, right?"

"Right. Her planet was called Florum. They were the enemy of the Gizzida, and Selena was taken prisoner. She's one of the nicest people you'll ever meet."

Colbie pulled Jess back into conversation.

"You got a clean bill of health?" Jameson asked.

"I'm fine. That damn monster was a pain in the ass."

Jameson swirled his glass of beer. "They all are." He

paused. "Those suckers were hiding in the sand, waiting to ambush us."

I felt a skitter of unease. "Yeah."

"I hope Jess can help us understand what the hell is going on with them lately."

Jess lifted her empty glass. "Who needs another drink?"

"Yeah, the next round is on the newbie," Marc cheered.

"Only if you don't call me newbie." She headed to the bar.

I watched her. I liked the way she walked. She was wearing dark jeans that hugged her curves, and a tight, red T-shirt. Her black hair was in its usual ponytail.

Jameson and Zeke were talking, and I tuned out their conversation as I listened to Kai move onto a new song. This one was more upbeat and a few people got up to dance.

I looked back at the bar, wondering where Jess was. I wondered if she needed some help with the drinks.

Then I stiffened.

She was leaning against the bar, laughing with some muscle-bound guy I didn't know. Maybe he was one of the firefighters? I'd seen him in here a few times. He was always charming a different woman. The man touched Jess' arm, and she smiled and nodded.

I scowled. I...didn't like it.

I rose to go and intervene. I was just looking out for her. She was new here. But before I'd taken a step, she grabbed a tray of drinks off the bar, smiled at the douche again, and headed back toward our table.

Relaxing, I sat down and blew out a breath.

Jess Ramos didn't need me to look after her. She could look after herself.

And if I tried, I suspected she'd punch me.

Jess

SIPPING MY BEER, I listened to the chatter of my squad.

I really liked Sasha and Colbie. They were lots of fun, and, added to that, they were great at their jobs. I could tell that Marc was the heart of the squad, and everyone looked to Jameson as their leader. North was a good medic, but he had spent the last hour scowling at me across the table.

I turned my glass around, fiddling with it. I wanted him to like me, dammit. Dad would tell me that it would all be fine. That I just needed to earn his trust.

We'd worked well together today. I just needed to give it time.

I rose. "I'm heading to the ladies' room."

I headed toward the back of the bar, and quickly visited the restroom. After I washed my hands, I walked out, and spotted Hemi Rahia behind the bar. Or rather, heard him.

He had a booming laugh. I'd heard all about him and the berserkers. Wild tales of their exploits during the fight with the Gizzida.

"There you are." The man I'd been talking to at the

bar appeared. Blake. He had a friendly smile and was nice to chat with. He was a firefighter for the town of Dawn and the surrounding communities.

"Hey," I said.

"I wanted to see if you'd like to dance?"

On the small dance floor, a few couples were moving around to the music.

I smiled. "Sure." I was new here and I wanted to make friends.

He reached out and took my hand.

Kai was playing a fun upbeat song on the piano. We found a spot on the dance floor and started to move.

Blake wasn't bad on his feet. He twirled me out and back in, and I laughed. He seemed nice, but my mind kept returning to the fight this morning. To the monsters we'd fought. I was eager to find some quiet time to take more notes on the creatures. If we encountered them again, I wanted to take a sample of the poison in their backs. I'd already talked to Jameson about getting my hands on a small test kit to take out with me. I was also very curious about how they'd lured us into a trap.

They certainly appeared to be working together. The monsters here were changing behaviors. More so than anything I'd seen back home.

It couldn't mean anything good.

"I'm cutting in," a deep voice said.

I looked up into North's blue eyes and stiffened.

"Ah, we aren't done yet, mate," Blake murmured.

"Yeah, you are," North said curtly.

"Blake, this is North, one of my squad mates," I said.

Blake didn't look happy, but he stepped away.

I managed a smile.

Then North wrapped his arms around me. He was taller and broader than Blake. He smelled like shower gel. Something crisp and fresh.

"How are your burns?" he asked.

I tried to focus. I hated that his proximity affected me so much. "They're fine. A little tender." Which he already knew from our trip to the infirmary. "You?"

"I'm good."

We were quiet for a moment, swaying to the music.

"Is that why you came over here? To check on my injuries that you know are healing fine?"

"Yes." His brows drew together. It was so annoying that a scowl made him look even more handsome. "And to warn you. That guy you were dancing with, he's here with a different woman every time I see him."

I raised a brow. "Are you warning me off Blake?"

North's jaw tightened. "I'm just looking out for a squad mate."

"Do you warn the guys off women?"

His scowl deepened. "I'm just trying to help."

"I'm a big girl, Connors. I've taken care of myself a long time."

"Fine."

But he didn't let go and we kept dancing. Our bodies brushed, and he was just so close. Warmth trickled through me.

His fingers flexed on my hip. God, we moved well together. In sync.

I looked up, and everything in me turned electric.

He was staring down at me, and I felt caught in that

blue gaze. His head lowered a little, and I felt like I was trapped in a spell.

Crash.

Shouting broke out nearby. I jolted. Two men were swinging punches at each other. Okay, technically, one was swinging, and the other was swaying. He'd clearly had too much to drink.

North squeezed my arm and strode over.

I watched Hemi leap over the bar in a smooth, athletic move. "Hey! Cut it out."

The men kept going at it. One fell and hit his head on a chair, blood trickling down his face. He jumped up to head back into the fight, but Hemi and North pulled the men apart.

"Cool it," Hemi bellowed.

"That's a nasty cut." North made the bleeding man sit in a chair. "Hemi, where's your first aid kit?"

"Behind the bar. Hang on, I'll get it."

I watched North tend to the man, talking in a calm voice. He got the drunk to settle down, then expertly cleaned and treated the wound.

Why did I find that just as sexy as dancing with him? Apparently, competence did it for me. I closed my eyes for a second. He was a squad mate. I wasn't here to get involved with anyone.

I was here to work and study monsters. To be a part of Hunter Squad.

I was not messing that up by getting involved with one of the men on my squad. It didn't matter how attractive or intelligent he was.

If Dad knew, he'd be spitting mad.

Don't get distracted by a pretty face, Jessie girl. Hormones fade and then you're left with broken pieces.

Besides, I wasn't even sure if North Connors liked me.

I shook my head and made my way back to our table.

"Never a dull moment at Hemi's," Colbie said, as she dipped a corn chip in some guacamole.

I managed a smile and sank back down in my chair.

CHAPTER FOUR

North

Night had fallen. The crowd at Hemi's had grown exponentially, and the noise and sea of bodies ebbed around us as we headed out.

The squad all called out our goodbyes to each other.

"Jameson." A blonde woman ran down the sidewalk.

Our squad leader's rugged face lit up. "There she is." He scooped up his girlfriend Greer, and then they were kissing.

"You're back," he said.

"I am." She wrapped her legs around his waist.

"How's your dam, Greer?" Marc called out.

"Monster free." She grinned at us.

"You're welcome," Marc said. "I was excellent bait."

Hunter Squad had taken down an aquatic monster that had been in the dam and attacking the workers. It had killed some of Greer's engineering team. Jameson and Greer had almost lost their lives trying to kill it. And

Marc had been seriously injured while dangling from the Talon.

Colbie snorted. "The monster didn't even try to eat you. It knew you'd taste bad."

"Lark, I promise I'm tasty." He winked.

"Night." Jameson carried his woman down the street. "See you all tomorrow."

I shook my head, still surprised at how happy the two of them were. I fell into step with Jess.

She shot me a look.

"I'm walking you home," I said.

"Your place isn't in the same direction as mine."

"It's not far."

"I thought Dawn was safe."

"It is."

She shook her head. "Whatever, Connors."

We were quiet as we left the shops and restaurants behind, and walked into the quiet streets, lined with eco-houses.

"Have you settled into your place?" I asked.

"Mostly." She tucked a loose strand of hair behind her ear. "I didn't bring too much stuff with me, so Jameson arranged a place with some furniture. Lucky, otherwise I'd be sitting on the floor."

I nodded. "My mom helped me set up my place when I first moved out."

"Your parents live in Dawn?"

"Yes, but they're away on a trip right now."

Jess slid her hands into her pockets. "Your dad was a berserker."

"He was. And mum's a tech geek."

"How did they meet?"

I grinned. "Online gaming."

Jess smiled back. "I sense a good story."

"Yeah. I'll tell it to you one day."

We turned a corner, the path bringing us right up to the wall that surrounded Dawn. Jess arched her head and looked up. "I hope that one day, we no longer have to wall in our towns."

"One day." I paused and took her hand. "Come with me."

I walked us over to the nearest guard tower, then nodded at the guard on duty. "Hey, Tom."

"North."

"We're just going to take a peek."

The older man gave me a chin lift.

We climbed up the stairs to the top of the wall.

On top, we had a view of the surrounding rolling hills, doused in moonlight. There was a glimmer of brighter lights to the north. New Sydney. Stars twinkled overhead.

"Wow." She looked up. "Before the invasion, you had to travel far out of the towns and cities to see the stars. There was too much light pollution, otherwise. All the stars are so different here in the southern hemisphere."

"That's Orion." I pointed. "And the Southern Cross." Something caught my gaze. I glanced down to the field below us, and I saw movement in the shadows below. "We have a visitor."

Her expression sharpened. "It's a monster."

It was too dark to tell exactly what it was. It didn't seem to be coming any closer. "Yeah, there are always a few hanging around. Testing the walls. The guards have a thermal camera, so they'll be keeping an eye on it. If any monsters get too close, the guards will fire on them and chase them off."

She nodded, thoughtful.

"You really like to study them?"

Her face brightened. "I do. There are so many different types, with different behaviors, different breeding habits." She paused. "In the decade after the invasion, people thought the monsters' behavior was completely random, but certain traits were already obvious." She made a face. "There have certainly been some changes in their behavior recently."

"I don't want to believe that they're working together, but I know that they're not just dumb, mindless beasts. I've seen that for myself." I scanned the surrounding hills again.

"That's New Sydney?" She pointed to the lights in the distance.

"Yes. Most of the city was destroyed. A large alien ship landed there during the invasion. The ship's been dismantled now, and the tech analyzed."

She nodded.

"The New Sydney community was set up in the city center. That's where the Eastern Australian Council is based. They provide leadership for the eastern half of Australia. They oversee Squad Command, the Education Board, the Manufacturing Division, and the Agricultural Department. Most small communities have local leadership, but they all check in with the council. Share resources and ideas. Help each other out."

"My cousins, Uncle Cruz's daughters, both work for the council."

My lips quirked. "Bryony does a bit more than work for them. She's president and an excellent, thoughtful leader."

"Cruz and Santha are so proud of her."

Cruz and his wife Santha had saved a young Bryony in the middle of the invasion and adopted her.

"And he says that Kari will probably take over from her one day," Jess continued.

I had no doubt. Kari Ramos was smart, driven, and a workaholic.

There were some lights closer to the east of Dawn. "That's Squad Command." Our headquarters were a short drive from the town. "Come on. I promised to walk you home."

We were quiet as we descended the wall and headed down the street. It was empty, and most of the lights were off in the surrounding houses.

Soon, Jess stopped and walked up a short path. Her wooden house looked the same as mine. It had an angular, black roof, and wooden siding. The roof absorbed sunlight during the day and generated power. There were some green plants in a large planter by the front door.

She hadn't left any lights on and the house was draped in shadows.

She turned to face me. "Well, thanks for walking me home, and for the stargazing."

I nodded and slid my hands in my pockets. I felt...

Hell, I didn't know what I felt. I just knew that Jessica Ramos unsettled me.

She stepped closer and I smelled her perfume. Something with a lush, sexy undertone.

"Good night, North."

"Night." I lowered my head and pressed a kiss to her cheek.

She stilled. I stilled. My lips were touching soft skin.

Then she made a sound.

A soft, hungry sound.

My gut clenched, and I dug deep for some control. But I still let my lips ghost over her skin. Her hands tangled in the front of my T-shirt.

Then she turned her head. Our gazes connected, just as her lips touched mine.

I heard something inside me snap like a rubber band. Then my mouth was on hers—hot and hard. I kissed her, and she returned it just as eagerly.

Before I knew it, our tongues were tangling and I lifted her off her feet.

She let out a husky sound and wrapped her legs around my waist. I slid my hands around to cup her curvy ass.

I took two steps, and her back hit the front door.

Then I devoured her.

Jess

GOD, the man could kiss.

I surrendered to it. I stopped thinking and worrying and overanalyzing. My tongue stroked his and I slid my fingers into his thick hair. North tasted like sin and the best mistakes. For the first time in a long time, I just let myself feel.

There was no work. No grief. No worry. Just pure desire.

It felt so good.

His hard body pinned me to the door. I slid my hands to his broad shoulders, kneading the muscles that I found there. I moaned. He was all hard muscle.

"Jesus... Jess." His mouth moved to my neck and pleasure shot through me.

With a cry, I arched into him. "Inside," I panted.

"What?"

I fumbled for the door and slapped my hand to the lock.

I heard it beep and the door clicked open. We stumbled inside. North caught me so we didn't fall. I already knew he had strength and good reflexes.

He slammed the door shut, and then I was pinned to the wall beside it. We shared another deep, sexy kiss. I was going up in flames.

A tiny voice in my head was trying to tell me to slow down, but I ignored it.

I wanted to feel.

I wanted pleasure.

I wanted North.

I tugged at his shirt, suddenly desperate for skin. He disconnected our mouths long enough to rip the T-shirt over his head.

Oh wow.

In the low light, I saw the perfection of his chest and abs. Every muscle was defined. There was a tattoo, but I couldn't quite make it out in the darkness. I touched a line of dark ink.

He sucked in a breath. His hands were on my T-shirt and then it was gone, and I was just wearing my black bra. I was glad I'd worn my nice set tonight.

He gave a low growl, then his mouth closed over my nipple, sucking it through the lace. I moaned, electric tingles skating though me.

"So sweet," he said. "I wonder where else you're sweet."

My belly clenched and filled with delicious flutters. It had been a long time since a man had turned me on this much.

He sucked on my other breast until I was gasping for air. My nipples were hard and aching.

Then he let my feet touch the floor. Before I could say anything, North dropped to his knees in front of me.

Oh. My belly swooped.

He undid my jeans, then pulled them and my panties down my legs. He pressed a kiss to my hipbone, then lower, on my thigh. My chest was rising and falling fast. I hadn't realized that the sexiest thing in the world was North Connors on his knees in front of me.

He parted my legs, and wrapped one of my thighs over his shoulder.

God. North's dark head was between my thighs. I ached, and the anticipation left me jittery. "North... Please..."

His hands wrapped around my thighs, then he pulled me closer and buried his face between my legs.

"Oh, *God*." As his mouth touched my swollen flesh, sensations rocketed through me.

His fingers dug into my skin as he licked and sucked. His tongue lapped, then touched my clit. I jerked, my hands tangling roughly in his hair.

I was out of control. Desire, pleasure, and need were a potent mix. I ground my hips against his face.

His fingers bit deeper, and I knew I'd have bruises. I liked the thought.

He growled, and that deep masculine sound vibrated through me. When his clever, relentless lips closed over my clit, I whimpered.

I was on sensation overload. My orgasm hit—hard and blindingly fast. I cried out, squeezing my thighs around his head.

He groaned, eating me with his sinful tongue as I shook. Panting, I came back down and tugged at him to get up.

I'd come, but I still felt achy and empty. He rose in front of me, heat pumping off his bare chest. I frantically worked the button and zipper of his cargo pants open and pushed his dark boxer shorts down.

And freed the most beautiful cock I'd ever seen.

I sucked in a sharp breath. It was long, the perfect girth, and even looked good—smooth and sexy.

Like him.

I wanted that cock inside me. "Now, North."

He stepped closer. His hard chest pressed against me, and that impressive cock dug into my belly. He lifted me, and a thrill ran through me. I found myself pinned against the wall again, my legs wrapping around his lean waist.

"You want me to fuck you?" His voice was low.

"Yes."

"How, Jess? Slow and teasing? Hard and fast?"

"Hard. Fast." My heart knocked against my ribs.

"Good." I felt him fist his cock between our bodies, the swollen head brushing between my legs.

He thrust inside me.

I let out a cry, and it meshed with the small groan that exploded out of him. My nails dug into his shoulders as I absorbed the pleasure-pain burning through me. I was so full.

"I can feel how wet you are." His voice was a gritty growl. "How tight."

His voice made me tighten my legs around him. "Fuck me, North."

"Yes, ma'am." He cupped my ass, pulled out, then slammed back in. He worked his big cock inside me until we were both slick with sweat and panting.

I never wanted it to stop.

His mouth was on mine—a mindless, passion-filled kiss. My climax shimmered, I was on the edge.

"Come on my cock, Jess. *Now*."

Those words tipped me over the edge. I screamed, and sharp-edged waves of pleasure hit.

A moment later, he thrust into me and stayed there. He groaned, his big body shaking as he came deep inside me.

Small aftershocks of pleasure shivered through me.

My brain needed a reboot, because it certainly wasn't functioning. We stayed there for a minute or three, who knew how long? It was lucky, because I was pretty sure my legs would collapse without him holding me up.

Finally, he set me on my feet. Our gazes met.

And reality—that sneaky bitch—hit me like a monster at full speed.

I'd just fucked a squad mate.

I was the new member on the team, the only female soldier on the team, and I'd screwed up. It didn't matter how much I'd wanted it or how good it had felt. I couldn't let this get messy. I couldn't let it ruin things.

I cleared my throat. "That was really great, North."

His gaze narrowed and he cocked his head. "Great?"

"Yes. We clearly needed it." I straightened and realized I was only wearing my bra. *Dammit*. I snatched my shirt off the floor. "The moment we met, we both know there was a...spark." I pulled my shirt over my head. "Now, we've gotten it out of our system." I pasted on a big smile. "Now we can get on with things."

"Get on with things?" He stared at me with an unreadable look.

I nodded.

His chest rose and fell, and I tried not to get distracted by the muscles and ink. "If that's what you want."

"Yep," I said brightly.

He turned away and started pulling his own clothes back into place. He yanked his shirt over his head. He shot me one long look, then turned and stalked out.

Shit.

I closed the door behind him and sagged against it. I pressed my cheek to the cool wood, my pulse still racing.

I had no idea what I wanted.

And I wasn't exactly sure how we'd left things.

But standing there with North's come sliding down my thighs, I had to admit that I was pretty damn confused.

CHAPTER FIVE

North

The next morning, I hurried into the squad room. We'd gotten a call out.

I'd spent the night trying *not* to think of Jessica Ramos. Definitely not thinking of her tight pussy, her sweet cries, or the scratches she'd left on my back.

I turned the corner, and heard my squad talking. Marc's voice was louder than the rest, and he was yammering on about something.

Then I saw Jess. My insides locked.

Everyone stood at their lockers, strapping on their armor and checking their weapons. Jess was sliding a knife into the sheath on her thigh. The thigh that had been wrapped around my head while I'd eaten her last night.

"Hey," Jameson said. "There you are. I was about to send out a search party."

I gave him a chin lift.

Jess looked up, and our eyes locked for a second before she looked away.

"Did you get lucky, Connors?" Marc asked, grinning at me. "You look...different. And you're never late."

"I'm here, and where I put my dick is none of your business." I opened my locker.

"Ooh, I take it back. You're too uptight to have gotten lucky."

I toed off my shoes and tossed one at him.

Marc dodged with a laugh.

I methodically pulled my armor and combat boots on, then got my medical backpack out. I'd already re-stocked it, I did that every time we returned from a mission, but I still always double-checked it before we headed out.

"Okay, everyone, listen up," Jameson said.

We all gathered around.

Jess stood beside me, and I tried not to notice her proximity. It was impossible. I could smell her, hear her breathing.

Out of our systems, my ass.

Jameson's rugged face was set in serious lines. His gaze flicked to me for a second, then Zeke, before he looked at the others. "We have two children missing from the town of St. Albans."

My gut curdled. Old memories scratched at me with sharp claws.

"The two boys are ten and eleven. Their names are Joe and Hudson. They snuck out past the town wall, and some of their belongings were found abandoned in a field." He paused. "There were monster prints nearby."

"Jesus," Kai murmured.

Across from me, Zeke sucked in a deep breath. He'd been snatched by a monster when he was twelve. He'd survived, but he never, ever talked about it.

"We're not giving up hope." Jameson looked at me again. "We're going to do everything to find them and bring them home to their families."

One way or another. I heard the unsaid words. I nodded.

"Zeke, you good?" Jameson asked.

The tall man's chin lifted. "Yes."

Our leader nodded. "Let's move out."

I turned back to my locker. I remembered another boy. Hurt and scared. I'd promised to help him... And I'd failed.

"North?"

Jameson stood behind me. The locker room was empty, and I realized the others had gone to the Talon.

"I'm okay, Jameson. This brings up some bad memories, but I'll do my job."

"I know. These kids could still be alive."

I hoped they were. I pulled my medical backpack on.

Side-by-side, we walked out to the hangar. There were several quadcopters parked in a row. Colbie was already in the cockpit of our Talon. She waved at us through the glass, and Jameson and I climbed aboard.

"Prepare for takeoff," Colbie said.

I sat, and a moment later, a siren sounded. I knew the roof overhead was retracting. The Talon lifted off.

As soon as the Talon cleared the base, I stared down at the green fields around us. The aircraft swiveled and we headed north. St. Albans was a small, inland town, north of New Sydney.

"Any description on the monster that took the kids?" Jess asked.

Jameson shook his head. "No one saw it. They sent through pictures of the prints." He pulled out his communicator, and tilted it so we could see.

My gut hardened. *Hell.* It was big. The print had three huge claws and made me think of fossilized dinosaur tracks I'd seen in images.

"They said there was a pungent smell," Jameson added. "Like rotting mud."

Jess nodded, and made some notes on her own communicator.

I turned my head to look out the window. I wasn't sure if I was hoping the kids were alive, or had been given a quick death. Monsters could cause a lot of damage without killing.

Old memories pushed at me again, but I ruthlessly locked them down.

I needed to focus on saving these two boys, not thinking of the one I hadn't saved.

Jess

I'D KNOWN that seeing North this morning would be awkward.

It was weird. I was sitting across from him, and all I

could think about was the fact that he'd been inside me, that he'd made me come. My belly filled with heat.

I swallowed, and stroked the cool metal of my carbine. I'd expected some glares or something, but all I'd gotten were a few long gazes, and now he seemed preoccupied.

Next to him, Zeke's face was totally blank. He was usually hard to read but right now, I got nothing off him.

"Marc?"

"Hmm." My squad mate was sitting beside me and gave me a small smile.

"Why did Jameson ask if Zeke was okay with this mission?"

Marc's smile faded and he glanced at his brother. "Zeke got snatched by a monster. He was twelve. He made it, but…"

I saw a terrible darkness flit through Marc's eyes. It had to have been hard on Zeke and on Marc.

"Don't worry, I'll keep an eye on my bro," Marc said. "He'll do everything he can to save those boys."

I glanced at North again. "Is North okay?"

Marc blew out a breath. "When it's kids, it's tough on him." He leaned in closer, keeping his voice low. "On an early mission, he rescued a boy. A teenager. A monster had torn the kid up really badly, and the boy was terrified. North did everything he could, but…the kid didn't make it."

"Oh." I glanced back at North. His jaw was so tight it looked like granite, and I wanted to touch him, comfort him.

I curled my fingers into my palm.

He wasn't mine to touch or comfort. We were colleagues. Squad mates. We couldn't be more than that, no matter how good the sex was.

I was here to be a member of Hunter Squad. I was going to expand my monster research. I'd promised my dad on his deathbed that I'd do this, and live to the fullest.

He'd been so proud of my work.

"You can see New Sydney below us."

I startled and looked at North. He tilted his head toward the window.

I shifted over and looked out. *Oh.*

Ruined buildings filled the landscape below us. Just ahead lay what remained of the city center. There were still some skyscrapers standing, while others were in tatters. One section of the city was different. It was surrounded by a sturdy, metal wall. The streets were clear of debris, and the buildings were lower and looked newer. One looked grander than the others, with a domed roof. I assumed this was the rebuilt center of New Sydney.

Then the Sydney Harbor Bridge came into view. It was broken, the two sides no longer meeting over the water.

Wait. I leaned closer to the window. There were workers on the structure. A large crane was set up on the northern side.

"They're rebuilding the bridge?"

"Yeah," Jameson said. "It's the main access across the harbor north and south. Right now, people have to fly or take a boat across. Plus, it's also a symbol. That things can be rebuilt."

My gaze drifted over the water of the harbor as it stretched eastward toward the ocean. Then, the city center was gone, and there were more ruined suburbs below. Every now and then, I'd spot a lone building that seemed untouched by the chaos.

We continued north, and soon we moved over a dense spread of trees. Ahead was a large river.

"This was all national park," North said. "And that's the Hawkesbury River."

"We took down some monsters hanging in the river last year," Marc said. "They kept stealing cattle from a nearby town. They were holed up in the rusted shipwreck of an old Australian Navy ship from the 1900s."

The Talon changed directions, following a smaller tributary of the larger river.

"St. Albans ahead," Colbie said.

"Jameson," Sasha's voice came clearly over the comm line. "The town leader is waiting for you, her name is Danielle. Along with her head of security, Garth. They'll meet you on arrival."

A small, walled township nestled beside the curve of a river came into view. The land around it was hilly, and quite pretty; green and lush. Some smaller, walled enclosures sat outside the town proper, and I realized that they were for livestock.

A group of people was waiting outside the gates for us. Several guards stood nearby, weapons in hand. The Talon descended and landed.

I followed the others off the aircraft. A woman with steel-gray hair stepped forward. She looked like she was in her mid-sixties, and her gaze shone with sharp intelligence.

"Hunter Squad, I'm St. Albans town leader Danielle Fraser."

"I'm Jameson Steele." Jameson shook the woman's hand. "Tell us everything, so we can get started."

She nodded. "The boys snuck out early, before school. They found a spot where they could get through the gates." She huffed out a breath. "They're both bright, curious, and adventurous. Too adventurous."

"You found some of their gear?" Jameson asked.

She nodded. "We believe they were going to see some of the livestock."

"Show us the area where you think they might have been taken."

A tall man stepped forward. "I'll take you. I'm Garth Stevens, Head of Security for St. Albans."

"How long have they been gone?" I asked.

"They were discovered missing when they didn't turn up to school." Grim lines bracketed Garth's mouth. "Their parents were working. The boys have been gone for over four hours."

Shit. That was a long time.

"Is that them?" a woman's sharp voice said.

We all looked up. A frantic woman, along with a couple, was pushing out the gates toward us.

The woman's face was lined with fear and worry. "You're going to find Hudson? He's my only child. He's all I have."

The couple grabbed her, and the other woman

hugged her. The man was tall and slim, and kept his arm around both of them.

He looked over. His shirt was rumpled and his hair messy, likely from running a hand through it. "Our son Joe is missing, too. He and Hudson are best friends."

"We'll do everything we can to bring them home," Jameson said.

I glanced at North. There was a desolate look in his eyes, and I took a step toward him.

His gaze sliced my way and his face shuttered.

"We're going to find them," I said quietly.

He gave a brief nod. "We'll try."

We followed the head of security through some trees. There was a round enclosure near the river, filled with mooing cows.

"The Macdonald River has created excellent farmland," Garth said. "People have been farming here for hundreds of years, I—" He gripped the back of his neck. "Please find the boys."

That's when I saw the shoe in the grass by the cows. A kid-sized running shoe. Nearby, there was a comm unit with a cracked screen and a toy. I crouched down. It was a small robot.

"They were taken here," Garth said.

I lifted the robot. The paint was worn off in parts. It was white with a touch of red. It was well-loved. *Oh, God.* The shoe was so small, and it made my heart squeeze. They were just kids, exploring, pushing boundaries.

Kai crouched and touched the monster print nearby.

"Looks like it was just one creature. Big. Carried both

boys." He rose and followed the trail toward the river. He paused and looked back. "I can track it."

Jameson nodded. "We'll find them."

Danielle nodded and wrapped her arms around her middle. "Please. They're good kids, and they don't deserve this."

"We'll do our best." Jameson turned and jerked his head. "Hunter Squad, move out."

I slipped the robot into my pocket. I was going to give it back to whichever boy it belonged to.

Kai took the lead, moving at a steady pace along the river, following the prints and signs. There were spots in which I couldn't see any trace, yet Kai knew where to go. He was good.

We crossed a green field, and I saw the ruins of a very old stone building. A chimney was still standing but the rest was rubble.

"Lots of old historic buildings from when the Europeans first settled here," North said.

We crossed through the river, splashing as we came out the other side. On this bank, the trees thickened. I looked up at some birds squawking in one of the trees. I was so busy admiring them, I tripped on a tree root.

A strong hand grabbed my elbow and caught me. I turned and looked at North. "Thanks."

He gave me one nod.

As he moved ahead, I still felt tingles from his touch. Then I remembered other places he'd touched me.

Jess, stop thinking about him.

Ahead, Kai paused. His brows drew together as he studied the ground.

"The tracks have stopped." Marc looked around. "The ground's really dry here."

No. I looked at the hills around us. We needed a trail, or we'd never find the kids.

Kai crouched and pressed his palm to the soil. He closed his eyes.

A minute passed, and Kai didn't move or say anything. Nor did the others.

"What's he doing?" I murmured.

North got a strange expression on his face. "He's reading the earth."

My brows drew together. "But there's nothing to read. There are no prints."

"No, he's not looking for prints. His mother is really connected to nature. He doesn't have her full abilities, but he can still...feel things. Through the earth."

My brows winged up. *Oh, wow.*

Then Kai rose and pointed. "They went that way."

CHAPTER SIX

North

Jogging through the trees, dappled sunlight flickered over us through the branches overhead. I really wanted to believe the boys were still alive.

But the longer it took us to find them, the odds decreased.

Kai jerked to a stop and cursed.

"Kai?" Jameson said.

Kai looked up. "Blood." He held up his gloved fingers; they were covered in red.

I stepped forward. The ground here was churned up, and as I scanned, I noticed several drops of blood on the dirt, splattering the dried leaves.

"It looks like one of the kids got free," Kai said. "Maybe scuffled with their captor."

"And got hurt." My jaw tightened. I kept trying to tell myself that this wasn't the same as Drew.

"The monster went that way..." Kai paused as he

pointed, a groove in his brow. "It looks like it was following a set of smaller prints, but the blood doesn't go that way."

I looked around. "One boy was injured, and the other ran. The monster could only follow one of them."

"Where did the injured boy go?" Jameson turned in a slow circle. "Everyone fan out."

We spread out, searching for more blood or any sign of the boy.

Where are you?

Ahead of me, Jess stopped by a fallen tree. The large trunk was now hollowed out and overgrown with bushes and grass. She pushed some of the vegetation aside.

"Hey." I grabbed her arm.

"What? This could be a perfect hiding spot."

"I know that we're usually more worried about monsters, but Australia is home to some of the deadliest snakes in the world. Taipans, brown snakes, red-bellied black snakes, death adders—"

She held up a hand. "I got it. Lots of killer snakes."

"I suggest you use a stick, not your hand." I grabbed a stick off the ground and held it out to her.

She took it and her nose wrinkled. "I'm not fond of snakes."

"And I'm not fond of treating painful snake bites."

She started poking inside the fallen trunk. "Ugh, there are lots of spiderwebs."

"Australia has lots of nasty spiders too."

"Yes, I know all about Australia's very large bug population." Suddenly, she gasped and leaped back, practically throwing herself into my arms.

An angry brown snake hissed and slithered out of the tree.

"Oh God," she whispered.

We watched as its long, thick, sinuous body slithered away.

"You okay?"

She scrambled away from me, patting her chest. Then she tightened her ponytail. "I'm fine." She shuddered. "I really hate snakes." Then she stilled. "North, look."

I turned and saw a small, bloody handprint on the fallen trunk of the tree. I touched my ear. "Jameson, we found a handprint. He came this way."

"Acknowledged," Jameson replied.

I leaped over the fallen tree and scanned the ground on the other side. I spotted some footprints—one with a shoe, and one of a bare foot. The poor kid was only wearing one shoe.

"This way."

Jess and I broke into a jog. We followed the prints until we reached another creek. The water rushed quickly past us, splashing over some rocks. The spot was almost idyllic.

"Do you see him?" I asked.

She shook her head.

"Come on." I moved down the bank and spotted more prints. "He swam across." I waded into the water.

The creek was deeper than the other one we'd crossed, and soon, the water reached my hips. I held my carbine above my head.

Jess sloshed through the water beside me, holding her weapon up, as well.

On the other side of the river, the footprints disappeared.

If I were a frightened, hurt boy, where would I go? I looked up. I'd try to climb a tree. But the kid was injured, so climbing might be too hard. We walked on. As I scanned around, I noted one of the large trees—a blue gum—was hollowed out at the base. A flash of red caught my eye and my pulse spiked.

I waved at Jess and pointed. We circled the tree, and found a young boy, huddled in a ball in the rotted-out hollow.

"Hey there," I said in a calm voice.

His head jerked up, his face dirty and tear stained.

"You're not the monster?" the boy said in a thready voice.

"Nope." I slung my carbine on my shoulder and crouched. "My name's North, and this is Jess."

"Hi." She smiled and gave the boy a wave.

"We're Hunter Squad."

His face changed. "Hunter Squad. You're here to save me and Hudson."

That made him Joe. "Yep. Are you hurt, Joe?"

He nodded. "It scratched me. It hurts. Real bad."

I held a hand out. "I'm a doctor. I can help."

"You need to help Hudson." Joe made a hiccupping sound. "The monster has him."

"We'll help him. But you first."

He put his hand in mine.

"Good man." I gently eased him out of the tree trunk.

Then he cried out and collapsed. I caught him and laid him flat on the ground. His leg was badly clawed. *Jesus.*

For a second, I was thrown back to trying to save another boy.

And failing.

"North?"

I met Jess' steady, supportive gaze. I dragged in a deep breath, then slipped my backpack off my shoulder.

"I'm going to give you a shot, Joe. It's gonna stop the germs and help with the pain."

"Okay." His voice was meek. "But you've got to save Hudson." Tears filled his eyes. "He saved me. He told me to run, and he made the monster go after him."

"He sounds like a good friend." I dialed up the injector and pressed it to his neck.

Then I started cleaning his wounds. His sniffles just about killed me.

"Hey, Joe." Jess ran a hand over his sandy hair. "I think I have something that belongs to you." She held up a small robot. It was white with some red stripes.

He gasped. "That's mine." His fingers curled around it. "Hudson has one too. We like to make them battle."

"You will again, buddy," Jess said.

Joe clutched the toy as I worked on his injuries, and gave Jess a tentative smile.

Running footsteps sounded behind us and Joe gasped, fear filling his face.

"It's okay," I reassured him. "It's just the rest of our squad."

Jameson and the others appeared. Joe's eyes went wide.

"Guys, this is Joe. He's being very brave. He said the monster took his friend Hudson."

Jameson's mouth flattened. "Marc and Zeke, I need you to take Joe back to town. We're going to get your friend back, Joe."

I finished tying off the bandage on Joe's leg. Then I lifted the boy and handed him to Zeke.

"North." The kid grabbed my arm. "Please. Please save Hudson."

I nodded, my heart squeezing. I didn't want to let him down...or make a promise I couldn't keep.

Jess

"OKAY, we need to track this monster and find Hudson," Jameson said.

Zeke, Marc, and Joe had left, heading back toward St. Albans. Everyone's nerves were at a fever pitch. We all knew the missing boy didn't have much time.

Kai circled around, searching for tracks.

"The tracks are muddied up. Like the monster wasn't sure what to do. It's agitated."

"We'll split up," Jameson said. "Kai and I will head upstream, North and Jess, you two go downstream."

I turned my head and looked at North. He nodded.

We set off. The creek was almost peaceful, but I knew what could be lurking close by.

"You were good with Joe, kept him calm." I admired North's skills. He could calm a panicked injured person so easily—adult or child.

"I just hope we can bring his friend home." There was a dark edge to his voice.

I paused. "We will."

His jaw tightened, and there was such an emptiness in his eyes before he looked away. "I failed once before, and a boy died."

"That's not your fault, North. The monsters are to blame."

"I was young and cocky. I was so sure I could save everyone."

And now, he was a diligent and dedicated squad medic. Who still wanted to save everyone.

"Why did you want to become a doctor?" I asked.

"My dad. He was the medic for the berserkers."

Ash Connors. I'd seen a picture of the man, and North looked a lot like him.

"He dreamed of being a doctor, but life made that too difficult. I guess I wanted to fulfill his dream."

"He must be proud of you."

"Yeah. He and mom are great. What about your parents?"

I looked away, staring blindly at the trees. "My mom died when I was young. She'd been injured during the invasion. She'd sustained shrapnel wounds and lost a kidney. She never really got her health back after that, and in those early days, medical help wasn't always available. Having me didn't help."

"I'm sorry."

"Thanks." I smiled. "Luckily, I had an awesome dad, and a big, extended family. Dad was in the military."

"So he must be proud of you."

"He was. He passed away last year. He'd be so excited I'm here, a part of Hunter Squad."

North looked at me, his gaze intense. Then he jerked, his gaze dropping. "Jess, look."

A perfect monster footprint, embedded in the mud at the water's edge. It was a match to the one that had taken the boys.

"It came this way." I scanned the water. The creek was wider and deeper here.

I froze. The woods were eerily quiet. No birds chirping. No chittering of small animals. Not even the buzz of insects. I gripped my carbine harder. "I think—"

Something burst out of the water and grabbed my ankle. Before I could react, I was yanked off my feet. The carbine flew out of my hands.

"Jess!"

I was dragged down the bank and into the water. It wasn't too deep, and I tried to grab on to rocks, anything. I kicked back and hit something solid.

Whatever it was, it tried to pull me deeper into the water.

Hell no, asshole. I kicked and thrashed. The monster released its hold on my ankle, and I splashed forward toward the shore.

A carbine fired, and I saw North at the edge of the river shooting at—

I rolled and gasped for air. My gut locked.

A humanoid monster stood in the center of the creek,

waist-deep in the water. It was beyond ugly. It looked like it was made of wood, with striated, bumpy, brown skin. It had bone-like plates on its face, and its eyes were barely visible, but I saw its mouth. Full of razor-sharp teeth. Instead of hands, it had wicked claws. It was big, well over six feet tall.

North fired again, but the laser seemed to bounce off the hybrid.

"Jess!"

"I'm okay." I scrambled back to the riverbank.

"It's a river wraith. We've come across them before." He kept firing, but the monster stepped closer, fighting off the impact of the laser. "The bone plating protects them from carbine fire."

"How do we kill it?" I crouched, fighting off a huge rush of adrenaline.

"A knife between the plating. Preferably in the middle of the chest."

Lovely.

Suddenly, the monster lunged for me again. I kicked at it and leaped to the side. I yanked my combat knife off my belt.

It made no sound. No growls or grunts, nothing. It was eerie. I felt it staring at me, fixated on hunting me.

I attacked, slicing my blade across the bone plating. It whirled, moving faster than I guessed it could. A claw scraped the back of my armor.

It dug in and dragged me back toward the water again. I heard North cursing.

Water closed over my head. It was dragging me along through the creek. My head broke the surface and I gasped for air. Then it tossed me, and I landed on the far bank.

I looked up, coughing. North was slicing through the water toward us. The monster was focused on me. I gripped the knife hilt. *Come on, asshole. A little closer.*

It opened its mouth. Yes, what big teeth you have.

The knife was ready. I saw the spot on its chest with the gap in the armor plating.

Just as I leaped up to attack, North tackled it from the side.

Dammit. They wrestled in the shallow water, and I splashed toward them. The wraith lifted North and tossed him into the center of the river.

"North!" I snatched my blaster off my belt and aimed. I fired to keep the monster distracted.

"I'm all right." North sloshed back to my side, water sluicing off him.

I shoved the blaster away. "I'm going to attack with—"

It lunged at us.

I lifted my knife. "I've got this." I took a step forward. This damn wraith was going down.

North suddenly shoved me aside and ran at it.

I hit the ground on my side. *Dammit.* I scowled and straightened, watching him ram his own knife between the creature's armor plating.

It fell back, black blood running down its abdomen. It still made no sound.

It slumped into the river, and the current washed the body away.

North glanced back at me. I glared back at him.

CHAPTER SEVEN

North

She was safe.

Chest heaving, I cleaned my knife in the water and turned to Jess. "Are you all right? Are you hurt?"

Jess glared at me and sat up. There was blood on her face from a small graze. "I'm *fine*."

I reached out, and she smacked my hand away. I frowned.

"What the hell was that?" There was acid in her voice as she shoved to her feet.

I frowned. I'd been so focused on getting her safe, and killing the wraith, I wasn't sure what was going on.

"What?" I said. "A monster attacked you. I wasn't going to stand by and watch. I helped you, saved you."

"I had a plan, Connors. I'm a fucking soldier. I was about to attack it, and you pushed me out of the way like I was some damsel in distress."

Shit. Had I? "Jess, we were in a fight for our lives, I—"

She stepped forward. "You think because we fucked, you can choose what I do or don't do? That I need a big strong man to protect me?"

I rubbed the back of my neck. I wasn't dumb enough to walk into that. "No."

"You didn't treat me like a squad mate, North. Definitely not one you trust."

I blew out a breath. *Shit.*

She whirled and stomped back up the bank.

Was she right? Hell, maybe my feelings had made me react and want to protect her.

I'd seen the dangerous monster that had just tried to drown her, and I'd reacted.

But I did trust her.

"Jess." I jogged after her.

"There you two are." Jameson appeared, Kai beside him. Our squad leader's brows drew together. "Did you take a swim?"

"A river wraith decided we looked tasty," I said.

Jess' back was stiff, her face set in unreadable lines.

"You both all right?" Jameson asked.

I lifted my chin. "Yeah."

Jess nodded.

"We saw footprints," I said.

"Show me," Kai said. "Because we found nothing."

We all headed back toward the creek. I kept one eye out for any more wraiths. They were usually solitary, but who knew what the monsters were up to lately?

Kai studied the print, then scouted around. "I found the trail!"

"Let's move," Jameson said.

The four of us took off at a jog into the trees. I ran behind Jess.

She didn't once glance my way. Shit, I needed to apologize. I hadn't meant to go Neanderthal on her. She really did mess with my head.

The trees thinned out, and we stepped over a fallen wire fence.

"Looks like an old farm," Jameson said.

The field ahead of us was filled with long, overgrown grass. I lifted my carbine. Anything could be hiding in here. In the distance, I spotted a small, abandoned house and some old, rusted metal sheds.

"Sasha, any heat signatures?" Jameson asked, touching his ear.

"Negative, Jameson," the comms officer replied.

We walked in a line through the grass.

"Kai, can you see anything in here?" Jameson asked.

"There are some flattened patches of grass." Kai stopped, then pressed his palm to the ground and closed his eyes. A second later, he said, "They came this way."

We kept walking. There was a hill ahead, topped with rocky outcrops.

"Where the fuck did it go?" Jameson muttered.

I took a step, and my boot sank down into the dirt, almost twisting my ankle. "Hell."

Jameson spun around. "North?"

"The ground isn't solid. Nearly twisted my ankle. Be careful."

"The ground's all churned up," Jess said.

Ahead of us, the earth was all upended and fresh, the grass ripped up.

"Shit," Jameson said.

"I don't like the look of this," Jess murmured. "I saw something similar to this back home. Mutated prairie dogs with alien DNA. They burrowed in and liked to pop up and attack anyone walking over them."

"Nice." Jameson kicked the dirt.

But nothing popped up to attack us.

"Let's skirt around it." A muscle ticked in Jameson's jaw. "We don't have time to investigate right now. Not while the kid is in danger."

We headed around the churned-up area. I scanned ahead of us, but saw no movement, no sign of any monsters.

We'd also lost the trail.

"Kai?" Jameson said.

Our tracker pulled a face. "Nothing. No sign of the monster."

Damn. I looked around. Maybe we'd gone in the wrong direction.

My throat tightened. I couldn't face Joe and tell him that we hadn't found his best friend. My gaze shifted to the hill, then I frowned. "Jameson, look." I pointed.

The others swiveled and stared up at the hill.

Jameson drew in a breath. "A cave."

There was a large dark entrance set in the side of the hill.

"The ground is rocky leading up to it," Kai said. "It could've obscured the monster's tracks."

"Let's check it out." Jameson headed up the hill.

I waved at Jess. "After you."

She spared me a sharp look, then stomped ahead.

I sighed and followed.

Jess

SO NORTH REALLY WAS JUST ANOTHER dick.

I picked my way up the rocky hillside toward the cave mouth. I remembered the men from my first squad who'd doubted my abilities, or felt the need to protect me. It had come with a lot of condescending and belittling remarks. It hadn't taken me long to teach them the error of their ways.

My gaze flicked to North, then away again. Honestly, this time, I was disappointed.

I continued on to the top of the slope, then stopped.

There was an intricate old buttress wall that had been built inside of the hill. A flat path cut across the other side of the hill, away from the cave. "Look at that." The brickwork was immaculate and neat. And old. It was coated in moss.

North stopped beside me. "It's part of the old convict trail."

"The what?"

"When the English set up a colony here in Australia, hundreds of years ago, they used convicts to build the Old Great North Road. It was a pretty amazing feat of engineering that linked Sydney with the northern Hunter region."

"Oh." I honestly didn't know a lot about Australia's pre-invasion history.

"We're nearly there," Jameson said.

"I see signs of the monster coming this way." Kai's voice rose with excitement.

We carefully approached the cave mouth and all lifted our carbines.

Jameson touched the flashlight on the shoulder of his armor. The beam of light illuminated the darkness ahead.

"Jesus," Kai muttered.

A sticky, weblike substance hung from the ceiling and coated the rocky walls.

"Please don't be hybrid spiders," North muttered. "They're the worst."

"Shh." Jameson yanked out his combat knife, then hacked a hole through the web. He shoved it aside and continued into the cave.

We continued on, Jameson and Kai taking the lead.

"Jess." North grabbed my arm.

I yanked away.

"Hey, I just want to apologize," he said quietly.

I blinked. "What?"

His face was in shadow. "You were right. I was out of line earlier. It was the heat of the moment. I was just focused on the fight, and getting you free of that monster. I know you have skills. I trust that you have my squad's back. Have my back."

I stared at him for a long moment, then I nodded.

He nodded back, then pushed on ahead.

He'd apologized. I hadn't been expecting that.

But I didn't have time to think about it right now. We had a monster and a kidnapped boy to deal with. I hurried to catch up with the others. But still, my brain tried to process it. Not many guys I knew were good with an apology.

"Form up," Jameson said.

We all focused on the cave. The web stuff was thicker here, and I saw that it was harder for Jameson to cut through it.

"Could the monster get through this?" North asked.

"Maybe it made it," Kai suggested.

Eww. That was a gross thought.

"The cave is wider ahead," Jameson said. "Let's—"

"Shh." Kai held up a hand, cocking his head. "Quiet."

We all stilled.

I didn't hear anything.

Then, came a faint noise. A moan, maybe? I tightened my grip on my carbine. "What is that?"

Another moan. Then what sounded like a sob.

Of a kid.

My pulse spiked. "It's Hudson."

Kai pulled out his knife and helped Jameson hack through the web. We pushed deeper into the cave. The sticky crap caught on my armor, and I grabbed it, trying to rip it off. It stuck to my gloves.

We couldn't risk calling out to the kid, and alerting the monster if it was close by.

Finally, we reached an open space. The web stuff was all over the walls.

"Shit," Jameson said.

We skirted a large rock. In a few places, the web stuff was dense, creating oval-shaped balls.

I frowned. "Is that web...coating something?"

North reached one of the thicker pod-like things. He cut it open with his knife.

A body fell out.

"Fuck," Kai cried out.

I leaped back.

The body was desiccated, the skin like leather. But I could tell it was a woman. She'd had lots of blonde hair.

"Shit." North crouched and touched her. "She was in some sort of cocoon."

"That's just wrong," Kai said.

Jameson was frowning fiercely. "How long has she been in there?"

"It's hard to tell." North shrugged. "My best guess is a month or so."

"H-help."

The small voice made me swivel.

North shot to his feet. "Hudson?"

"Yes. I am...here."

I shifted my shoulder, my flashlight shining against the far wall. I spotted a small cocoon. It was moving. "North, look."

We raced over. I saw the boy was only partially covered by the sticky substance. His face was still half visible.

North carefully cut into the sticky web with his knife. "Hey, Hudson. I'm North. We're here to take you home."

The boy gave a hiccupping sob. "You're...Hunter Squad."

"That's right," North replied.

"I told Joe you'd come for us. When the...thing took us." His voice cracked. "Joe. Is he okay?"

"We found him. He's safe. He's more worried about you."

"He's my best friend."

North cut Hudson free, and the boy slid out with a cry.

"Careful." North eased him onto his back. "It looks like your arm's broken. Let me take a look at you." With quick movements, North pulled his backpack open.

"North...the thing." Hudson's voice lowered to a whisper. "It's still here."

Shit. I whipped my carbine up. Jameson and Kai moved in with me, and we scanned the cave.

I half listened to North talking with the boy, using that calm, steady voice. Hudson's panicked tone evened out, and his voice got stronger. He was reacting to North's calming influence.

Then in the depths of the cave, a shadow moved. "Three o'clock," I murmured.

"I see it," Kai said.

The monster roared and charged.

The beams of light caught it. It had a tall, almost emaciated body, with dark, spongy black skin. There wasn't any fat on it, and the skin was stretched tight over corded muscles. There were no eyes, or mouth, just a smooth, eerie face that ended in a long snout.

I had no idea what animals they'd been created from. It looked like pure monster.

The three of us lit it up.

The creature screeched and its snout flared open like petals on a deadly flower.

Laser fire made the cave as bright as day. I kept my finger on the trigger, aiming at the creature's torso.

Soon, the monster fell. It landed on its knees, and let out a garbled roar, then it collapsed forward and didn't get up.

I stopped firing. I watched its body twitching.

Jameson strode up to it, then kicked the monster over onto its back. He fired right into its eyeless face.

"What the hell was that?" Kai said.

Jameson shook his head. "Haven't seen anything like it before. Jess?"

"No." It didn't resemble anything I'd seen.

"Call Colbie." North carefully wrapped Hudson's arm, pinning it to his chest. "We need to get him out of here."

Jameson touched his ear. "Sasha, we have the boy. He's alive. Send Colbie to get us."

"Were there any other people here?" North asked.

The boy shook his head. "No, just the monster. It got kind of blurry. Then when I woke up, I was stuck in that stuff." He shuddered.

"You're safe now." North ran a hand over the boy's mussed, dirty hair.

"I had Echo with me. I wasn't alone."

I frowned. "Echo?"

With his good arm, he fumbled in his pocket and pulled out a robot the same shape as the one Joe had. This one was white with blue stripes.

"He kept me safe. Me and Joe both have them."

"Kai, we need to bag the woman's body," Jameson

said quietly. "Jess, take some pictures of these cocoon things."

I nodded. "I'll grab a sample of the stuff as well." I pulled my small science kit off my belt.

North kept Hudson occupied while the men slid the desiccated body into a body bag. I took photos and samples, then nodded at Jameson.

North lifted Hudson into his arms. "You ready to go home, buddy?"

The little boy nodded. "Yes, please."

CHAPTER EIGHT

North

I talked quietly to Hudson as the quadcopter flew toward St. Albans.

The splint I'd put on his arm and the painkillers I'd given them had done the trick. There was color back in his cheeks and he chatted non-stop. I even got him to laugh.

"I've never been on a Talon," he said with awe.

"Cool, huh?"

He nodded. "Yeah."

I'd administered nano-meds. The tiny, medical machines were racing through Hudson's small body. I was also carefully monitoring his vitals. I'd had nano-meds a few times myself, and I knew that sometimes they could go out of whack and attack things they shouldn't. Doctors kept sharp eyes on patients while they had the treatment. It had only been in recent years that we'd been able to take nano-meds out in the field.

I ruffled the boy's hair and felt a shot of warmth. He was alive. *Thank God.*

I looked up, and my gaze locked with Jess' dark one.

Then Jameson sat down beside her, and I looked away, but I listened to them talk.

"What do you think about the cocoons we found?" Jameson asked her.

"Honestly, I've never seen anything like it," she replied. "It seems strange that the monster hadn't killed…" she glanced at Hudson "…its prey."

"Perhaps it was saving…the prey for later?" Jameson said.

"The woman was dead. She hadn't been eaten."

I frowned down at the floor. All of this left us with more questions than answers.

"You got enough pictures?" Jameson asked. "Of the cocoons and the woman?"

Jess nodded. "I'll run analysis on the cocoon substance and check my database for anything similar."

"I'll ask the leader of St. Albans if anyone is missing who matches her description."

"It's all very strange, Jameson. Monsters usually hunt when they need to feed, or they just attack for fun and leave the remains. It's a lot of trouble to take live prey." She frowned. "I haven't seen anything like this back home. And those monsters on the beach, they were definitely communicating and working together. Much more so than my studies on pack monsters in North America."

Jameson crossed his arms, his face tense. "So you think something's going on with our monsters here?"

"It looks that way, but I need more data."

"Well, we have no shortage of monsters. We'll get more data, whether we want it or not."

That was the truth. I hoped to hell Jess could find out what was going on.

Soon, the Talon came into land at St. Albans. As soon as we touched down, I saw Hudson's mother running toward us.

I lifted the boy and carried him out of the quadcopter.

"Huddy!" The woman was crying as her gaze locked on her son. Garth, the head of security, walked with her. Zeke and Marc stood nearby.

"Mom!"

"His arm is broken." I carefully handed him over to Garth. "He's had a dose of nano-meds. He's going to be fine."

"Thank you." Hudson's mom smiled through her tears. She clutched Hudson's hand. "Thank you, all of you."

Nearby, I saw Jess smiling.

It was a happy ending. We didn't always get them, so we had to savor them when we did.

"North?" Hudson called out. "This is for you."

He was holding out his small robot.

"That's yours, buddy."

"I want you to have it. Echo will help protect you when you fight the monsters."

I smiled and took the toy. "Thanks, Hudson."

With a nod, the mother and Garth walked away with the boy. He was already telling them all about his adventure. I shook my head. Kids were so resilient.

"Thank you." The town leader, Danielle, stepped forward. "I cannot thank you all enough for bringing the boys home safely."

"Danielle, we did find a body," Jameson said quietly.

Her brows drew together.

"A woman," I said. "My guess is mid-twenties to late-thirties. Long, blonde hair. I found a tattoo on her wrist. It looks like a butterfly."

The town leader's eyes went wide. "No. Melanie."

"She's been missing a few weeks?"

The older woman pressed a shaky hand to her mouth. "Melanie Wakefield. She was unhappy here. Chaffing at life behind the walls. She'd saved up and purchased a vehicle. She left for New Sydney three and a half weeks ago. We hadn't heard from her, but we weren't worried." Danielle closed her eyes. "She never made it."

"No," Jameson said. "She didn't."

"That poor young woman." The town leader's eyes opened. "It was the same monster that took the boys?"

"It looks that way."

She nodded. "So, its dead. You saved Hudson and Joe, and got justice for Melanie."

"We'll take her body with us for an autopsy," I said.

"Fine." Danielle glanced at the surrounding hills. "Don't bring her back. Bury her somewhere pretty."

It was a quiet flight home. Most of the guys were dozing, and Jess had her eyes closed, too.

I sighed. I felt...edgy. I should be elated that we'd found the two boys alive and gotten them home.

But my thoughts had turned to Drew. The boy I hadn't been able to save.

My hand curled into a fist, and I tried to relax. I knew I'd have nightmares tonight. Drew screaming in pain, me unable to help him.

The teenager dying in my arms.

I tapped a boot on the floor and that's when I felt a gaze on me. I looked up and saw Jess watching me.

She slid across the seats, then touched my hand. She must have sensed that I didn't want to talk. We just sat there, and she was a quiet, supportive presence beside me.

Before long, we came in to land at Squad Command.

"I like it when a mission ends like this," Marc said, leaping out of the Talon. "Kids alive, and us not covered in monster crud."

"You still need to shower," Zeke said. "You stink."

"So do you." Marc elbowed his brother.

"I need to debrief General Masters," Jameson said. "Clean up and go home. Good work, everyone." He looked at me. "Really good work."

The others headed for the locker room.

Jameson grabbed my arm. "North, you all right? I know this would've dredged up some memories."

I blew out a breath. "I'll get there." Hell, it was Zeke who should be messed up, not me. He'd lived through being kidnapped by a monster. I needed to get a damn grip on this.

My friend nodded. "If you need to talk, call me."

That wasn't happening. I knew he'd be busy with Greer. "Thanks, J."

The others finished up in the showers, and called out their goodbyes. I didn't see Jess anywhere. I stripped my gear off, taking my time. Then I finally stood under the hot water. I dipped my head and stood there for a long time, letting it pour over my head.

I watched the water circle down the drain, and wished the old memories and old pain were as easy to wash away.

Jess

I FINISHED SCRIBBLING my notes in my communicator, then closed my locker.

I'd taken a quick shower, then headed straight to the lab to get my samples analyzed. Squad Command had a well-equipped lab and excellent staff. They'd have some results for me tomorrow.

Those cocoons... I had to work out what the monsters were doing.

The sound of running water caught my ear. The shower was still on in the men's locker room.

I bit my lip. The others were gone, so I knew it was North still in there. I fiddled with the hem of my clean T-shirt.

Don't think about him wet and naked.

I knew something was off with him. He should be happy about saving the boys. They were alive because of him.

Go home, Jess. Don't get involved.

I blew out a breath. I was already involved.

I'd been involved the moment those blue eyes hit mine.

And definitely after we'd had a quickie against the wall in my living room.

The shower turned off and I tightened my ponytail.

But North didn't come out.

I moved to the shower room door. I saw him, with a white towel wrapped around his waist and his chest bare, sitting on one of the benches. The air was steamy and his hair was damp. I let myself take a second to look at the tattoo on his chest. It was a dragon. It was amazing black ink that hugged his muscles and wrapped around his back.

Then I focused on him.

The white towel looked stark against his tanned skin. His handsome face was blank, but tight. One hand was bunched up by his side, and the other was turning Hudson's small robot over and over between his fingers.

"North?"

He didn't move or look up. "I'm not good company right now, Jess."

I walked over and sat beside him. "I wasn't expecting witty conversation." I paused. "Do you want to talk about it?"

I didn't ask if he was okay. It was clear that he wasn't.

"I don't talk about it." His voice was tight. "Ever."

"Sometimes talking can help."

He grunted.

"You did good work today. Those boys are alive thanks to you."

"The whole squad helped save them."

"But you treated them. More than that, you kept them calm and relaxed. You have a gift. Those boys will sleep better tonight because of you."

Silence fell.

"What was his name?" I asked.

The silence stretched on, then North sucked in a breath. "Drew. He was sixteen." A harsh expulsion of breath. "He'd gotten his first, part-time job in the agriculture fields. He'd only taken it because he wanted to buy his girlfriend a gift." North rubbed his face. "A monster attacked and dragged him off. It took a while before anyone realized."

"Hunter Squad went to find him."

North nodded. "Jameson was the second in command back then. A guy called Rich was in charge. God. I'd just finished my medical training." He shook his head. "I thought I knew everything. I was cocky as hell, and I thought I was invincible."

"What happened?"

"We tracked the monster through the bush. There was a lot of blood, so I knew the kid was hurt badly. I just believed that if we found him, it would be fine."

"You found him." But everything clearly hadn't been fine.

"Yeah. We found the monster and killed it. It had been snacking on Drew before we got there."

My stomach did a sickening turn. "Oh no."

"He had deep bite marks, and his abdomen was a mess." North stared at the wall, lost in the old, painful memories. "He was in terrible pain, and I gave him painkillers to help. Back then, nano-meds weren't stable enough to have out in the field. If I'd had them then, I might've saved him. There was so much damage."

"It's not your fault, North." I gripped his arm. "You did everything you could."

"He knew he was dying. He cried and asked for his mom. I held him as he took his last breath."

I couldn't stand it anymore. I shifted close to him and wrapped my arms around him.

He was stiff in my hold, then he moved, dragging me closer and burying his face in my hair.

"He was only sixteen. A good kid. He had his entire life ahead of him. If only..."

"If only the Gizzida hadn't invaded. If only Drew hadn't been attacked by a monster. That was out of your control, out of everyone's control." I smoothed my hands up his back.

He didn't say anything else. We sat there, holding each other, until he finally sat back.

"I am sorry about today, Jess. With the wraith. I just wanted to keep you safe. But you're right, in that moment, I didn't trust you or your skills. I should have."

But he was trusting me here and now. Sharing his darkest wound and letting me comfort him.

"It's all right, North." I rose. "Trust is earned. I know that. Get some rest tonight."

He nodded.

I hoped he would. I hoped he went home and slept this off.

I headed into the locker room, and he followed. I tried not to drool over his abs and that tattoo. I wasn't sure what I liked most—the abs, his chest, or his muscular arms.

Maybe all of him.

I grabbed my bag and slung it over my shoulder. "Night."

"See you later, Jess."

I felt his blue gaze on me as I left.

CHAPTER NINE

Jess

Peering into the microscope, I studied the sample of the sticky cocoon substance. I wrote some notes on my communicator, then looked at the next slide.

Around me the lab was filled with the quiet murmur of voices from the lab technicians as they went about their work. Squad Command had a really good lab. It was well-equipped and staffed with smart people.

How were the monsters making the cocoons? Could they all create this substance? And why? That was really what was bugging me.

I glanced out the windows into the courtyard below. Squad Command was a squat building built of solid concrete. The upper floors had glass, but the lower levels had no windows. It was surrounded by a large wall with several guard towers. The place was monster proof. Down below, some trainee recruits were being put through their paces.

Hunter Squad hadn't gotten a call out today. I'd decided to come into the lab, and I knew the rest of the squad were here too, working out in the well-equipped gym. Except North. Jameson had mentioned he'd volunteered to do some extra shifts in the infirmary.

I wondered how he was doing. Had he slept?

He isn't yours to worry about, Jess.

"Ms. Ramos?" A female technician stopped beside me. "I forwarded the toxicology report you requested to your device."

"Thanks." I swiped my comm unit and found the report. *Hmm.* I studied it and frowned. The cocoon substance had some sort of unknown chemical in it. They speculated it was possibly a sedative.

Not a toxin. So the cocoons weren't designed to kill their prisoners.

"You look good in a lab coat."

I looked up at Marc. He was wearing gym gear and smiling.

"What's up?"

"The boss man sent me to get you. We have a meeting with the generals. They want an update on the freaky-ass cocoons."

I wrinkled my nose and grabbed my communicator. "I wish I had more to share."

"Anything is better than nothing."

"Have you seen North today?" I asked casually.

Marc sighed. "Yeah. He looked like hell."

I shoved my hands in my pockets. I really wished there was something I could do to help North.

"When we rescue kids, it just stirs things up for him," Marc added. "He'll be fine. He's tough."

We walked down the hall, then a moment later, a set of double doors whispered open, and we walked into the main command room.

One wall was all flat screens, showcasing maps, live feeds, and other data. A huge light table sat in the center of the space. The rest of the Hunter Squad stood around it. My gaze went straight to North and my heart squeezed hard.

He hadn't slept. He had dark circles under his eyes and looked exhausted. His gaze flicked to mine for a fleeting second before he looked away.

"Ah, Marc and Jess, thanks for coming," a woman said.

Dragging my attention off North, I focused on the woman and man standing on the other side of the light table.

They both wore navy-blue jackets with their rank insignia in gold on their chests. They were both generals.

I'd met them both a few times before, and would have recognized them anyway. General Roth Masters had been the leader of Squad Nine during the invasion. He was a tall, muscular man, with gray hair he kept buzzed short. He radiated authority but I got the impression that he'd happily wade into a fight if required. Before the Gizzida had come, General Avery Stillman had been a part of the United Coalition's Central Intelligence Agency. Her dark hair was up in a twist and she had high cheekbones I'd sell my soul for.

I also knew they were married.

"We need an update on what you found at St. Albans," General Masters said, his voice deep.

Jameson nodded. He gave the pair a quick mission recap then nodded at me. "Jess took some photos and samples of the cocoons."

I touched my communicator and images appeared on the surface of the light table.

"Jesus," Masters muttered.

General Stillman frowned at the images of the cave, tracing one of the cocoons with a finger. "You rescued a young boy from one of these and discovered the dead body of a woman."

"Yes," I replied. "Hudson had only just been partially put in the cocoon. The woman, Melanie Wakefield, had been missing from St. Albans for several weeks."

General Stillman shared a look with her husband, then looked back at me. I saw intelligence and determination. "You've run tests on the cocoon material. Did you find anything pertinent?"

"I'm still analyzing but it appears the substance contains some sort of sedative."

General Masters frowned. "To incapacitate prey."

I nodded. "Keep them calm. It doesn't appear to kill. I'm not sure why Melanie died."

"I spoke with the leader at St. Albans," North said. "Ms. Wakefield was a Type 1 diabetic. She was due to have her insulin implant renewed. My guess is her death could have been related to that. We'll know more after an autopsy."

General Masters scraped a hand over his short hair. "We have something else to show you."

"I had some of my team start working on this last night," General Stillman said. The light table filled with a large map of the region. Dawn was at the southern end, New Sydney in the center, the Blue Mountains to the west and St. Albans to the north.

Several gold dots appeared, scattered across the map.

Jameson's brows snapped together. "What is this?"

"Reports of missing persons from all surrounding communities in the area," General Stillman said.

My chest hitched. *What the hell?* "There are so many." I counted thirty-five dots.

Masters nodded. "If the monsters are responsible, then this was well-planned. They've only taken one person here and there, spread around the different communities."

"One person going missing, or believed to be attacked, wouldn't raise many alarms," Jameson said.

"And we don't have the sort of central databases law enforcement used to have prior to the invasion," Kai added. "No one noticed an uptick in disappearances."

"All within a hundred-kilometer radius." North pressed his hands to the table, his face grim in the glow of light.

"Jess?"

I met General Stillman's gaze. "Yes?"

"We need to work out what the hell is going on with these cocoons. What they do. What the monsters have planned."

I nodded.

"We've alerted all communities to inform us if anyone goes missing," General Masters added. "We will not stand by while these damn abominations pick us off one by one."

"We'll stop this," Jameson said darkly. "Whatever it is."

Both the generals nodded.

"If my team find any more intel, we'll pass it along," General Stillman said.

We filed out of the command room. I glanced back and saw Masters press a hand to his wife's shoulder. The connection between them, the sense of solidarity and support, was obvious.

"Stay sharp, guys," Jameson said. "We could get called out at any time. Everyone is on high alert."

"I'll get back to the lab." I needed to uncover everything I could on the cocoons.

"Catch you later, Jess," Marc said.

As the others headed down the corridor, I caught North's hand. He looked back and the deep grooves beside his mouth made my chest ache. "How are you?"

"Fine. I need to get back to the infirmary."

I frowned. "I thought you finished your shift."

"I offered to work an extra one."

I bit my lip. "North, you need some rest. Did you get any sleep last night?"

He shrugged a shoulder. "Better to keep busy." His gaze turned inward and he pulled in a breath. "Do you think any of those missing people are still alive?"

"I hope so."

He pulled his arm free. "I need to go. See you later."

I watched him disappear down the hall, worry

nipping at me. He was in a dark place and I wished I knew how to help him.

North

IT WAS RAINING.

I'd finished a second shift at the infirmary, until the doctor on duty had made me leave. He'd said he didn't need a walking zombie making mistakes. I'd gone home and stared at the four walls for ages, before I'd fallen into a fitful sleep on my couch.

The nightmare had woken me. Left me drenched with sweat and my heart racing.

I couldn't get Drew out of my head. Or the scent of blood and death.

Or the sinking feeling of helplessness.

More people were out there, in the hands of the monsters. Either dead, hurting, or trapped in a damn cocoon.

That was when I knew that I had to get out of my house. I'd walked the streets of Dawn for hours, avoiding anywhere that I might run into someone I knew. It helped that most people I knew were tucked up in bed asleep at this time of night.

Then the rain had started.

I was drenched. My clothes were soaked and water was dripping off me.

I didn't care. I kept seeing Joe and Hudson in my

head, but their faces always morphed into Drew's. They were covered in blood.

Then, I was holding those young boys, and instead of rescuing them, I watched them die.

I shook my head. They hadn't died. They were fine and with their families.

My fucking brain didn't care about logic.

I turned onto the next street. Ahead, lay the center of a small square. A statue had been erected there. It was made of bronze, and showed three men wearing armor. The men were all tall and muscular, holding carbines, and staring toward the north.

It was a memorial to honor the squads that had fought and beaten the Gizzida.

It was supposed to represent all the soldiers, but one definitely looked like Marcus Steele, another like Roth Masters—he'd been the leader of Squad Nine—and the final man was Tane Rahia.

They'd fought; they'd lost people. Zeke and Marc's uncle, also called Zeke, had been killed. There had been so much death.

But I knew my dad and the others had gone on with things. They'd found hope, they'd continued on, they'd lived their lives, and had worked hard to rebuild. They'd kept the monsters at bay until the next generation had been old enough to take over the fight.

They didn't wallow in nightmares, or wake up choking on screams.

I scraped a hand over my face. When I looked up, I found myself walking up another residential street. When I realized where I was, I sucked in a breath.

My gaze fell on Jess' place.

I should leave. I should walk home. I should take a hot shower and pour myself a whiskey.

But as though I was on autopilot, my feet carried me up the path to her front door.

Then I just stood there. I couldn't bring myself to knock. Hell, I shouldn't be here.

I didn't leave, I didn't knock, I just dripped on her front porch.

A second later, a light snapped on and the front door opened.

"North?" Jess stood in the doorway. She was wearing a dress—it was a cream color, with thin straps that showed off her toned shoulders, and a soft and flowing skirt that reached her bare feet. I hadn't seen her in a dress before. Hadn't realized her toenails were painted pink.

She took one look at me and concern creased her face. "God, you're saturated." She grabbed my arm. "Come in."

She tugged me inside.

"I shouldn't have come." I hadn't consciously meant to come to her.

"Quiet." She pulled me into the middle of the living room. "Stay there." She disappeared down the hall, but was back a moment later carrying two fluffy, white towels. She started wiping me down and drying off my hair.

"Shirt off," she ordered.

I obeyed. I tugged it over my head, then dropped it to the floor. It landed with a wet slap. She dried off my chest and back.

"I really like your tattoo."

"Thanks."

She wrapped a towel around my shoulders, then ushered me to a stool at the kitchen island. Her place was a near mirror image of mine, although the colors were different. Her home was brighter, decorated in shades of white and blue.

She circled the island and walked over to the food unit. She programmed it, and then I heard it ding.

"Drink this. No arguments." She pushed a mug across the counter.

I took it and felt the warmth on my palms. "Hot chocolate?"

She nodded. "With a whiskey addition."

I took a long sip, and it instantly warmed my cold insides.

She leaned against the counter. "You look like hell, North."

"Yeah." I felt it too.

"Double shifts in the infirmary were not a good idea."

"I tried to sleep..."

"But?"

"Nightmares." I scrubbed a hand over my face. "I don't get them much anymore, but every now and then, one sneaks up on me."

"I'm sorry. I guess rescuing those boys stirred things up, and news of all these missing people."

I grunted. "No, I'm sorry. I didn't mean to come here. I just ended up on your doorstep." I sipped again. "The last thing you need are my problems."

"Shush."

She moved behind me, then I felt small hands on my shoulders, and it almost made me jump.

"You're so tense. You need to relax, or you'll snap." She started massaging, her fingers digging into my tight muscles. It felt good and my head fell forward. She kneaded harder.

I groaned.

"Just let it go for a little while," she murmured.

I closed my eyes, and Jess filled my senses. The sweet, shower-fresh smell of her, the feel of her hands, the sound of her dress rustling.

She was good, smart, nice, real. Alive.

Much better than blood, grief, and old memories that never left me alone.

"There you go," she murmured.

"I wanted to save Drew. He was just a frightened kid." Dammit, I hadn't meant to let the words out.

Her fingers paused for a second, then resumed massaging. "I haven't known you long, but I have no doubt you did everything you could."

"He looked a bit like me." I closed my eyes tighter. "I wished he didn't die."

"I know. But you don't get to decide when it's someone's time to go. We can only try our best, North. No one can do more than that. You need to stop beating yourself up for something that was out of your control."

She stopped massaging and stepped in front of me. She was so damn pretty. Her dark hair was loose, and the freckles on her nose stood out. I wanted to count them all.

"I know," I said. "Most days, I know that. But sometimes..."

"Sometimes the crap we keep hidden likes to pop up and smack us in the face."

I nodded. "Thanks. I should get out of your way."

"No, it seems that I like you in my way."

I lifted my head.

She smiled, then reached up for the thin straps of her dress. She pushed them off her shoulders.

The dress slithered down her body and pooled at her feet, leaving her naked except for a tiny pair of white panties.

"I think you should stay," she murmured.

Jess

I WATCHED North's hungry gaze run over my body. He was looking at me like I was his lifeline.

Why did I like that so much?

The darkness in his eyes slid away. Exactly as I'd hoped. It was replaced by hot desire.

He reached for me and yanked me onto his lap. I straddled him, gasping. His trousers were damp, his skin was damp. I pressed my hands to his broad shoulders.

"You're so beautiful, Jess. I never get tired of looking at you."

He lifted me up, and then his hot mouth clamped over one of my breasts.

Sensation exploded inside me. In seconds, my

nipples were tight buds, and heat filled me. I'd gone from zero to a hundred in the blink of an eye. I never knew it was possible to want someone this much.

I writhed, feeling the hard bulge beneath me.

"*North.*" My head dropped back, and he switched to my other breast.

"You have no idea, Jess. No idea how much you affect me." He lapped at my stiff nipple before sucking it into his mouth.

I jerked my hips again, grinding down on his cock. "I have a hint."

He growled, then he kissed me. The taste of him flowed through me, making me gasp. Then, he pressed kisses to my cheeks, my jaw, my neck. "I miss you when we're apart. How is that even possible?"

My heart squeezed. I leaned into him and pressed my mouth to his. As we kissed, his hands—those hands I'd admired so many times over the last few weeks—roamed over my body. Neck, shoulders, breasts, sides, belly. Every caress set off shivers down my spine.

Then his hand was between my legs, sliding inside the already soaked fabric of my panties. My body jerked. A thick finger pushed inside me.

My lips parted, my hips pushed against his hand. It felt so good.

"You're so slick." He made a low, masculine noise. "You know how badly I want to sink inside this hot, little body?"

My heart hammered, need filling every cell, every pore. "As much as I want you inside me."

His fingers clenched on the side of my panties. "How much do you like these panties?"

"I have others."

He wrenched his hand and the fabric tore.

Butterflies went crazy in my belly. That was so hot.

Then he fumbled with his cargo pants and urged me up. I felt the brush of his hard cock between my legs. Anticipation made my belly clench.

We froze there, his cock notched between my thighs. My gaze was locked with his blue one.

"Do it," I murmured, digging my nails into his shoulders.

"Jess..." Then he pressed inside me.

My chest hitched, my pulse thudded in my ears like a drum.

He groaned, then thrust up, filling me to the hilt. I moaned. Nothing felt better than North Connors buried inside me.

We were joined. It was impossible to get any closer.

Gripping his shoulders, my fingers biting into his ink, I started to ride. I picked up the pace, and soon we were both panting, our bodies slick with perspiration. His hands clenched on my ass, working me faster up and down on his cock.

I ground my hips in a circle, needing more. "Rub my clit," I panted.

His hand channeled between us. Unerringly, he found the right spot. He put just the right amount of pressure on my swollen clit.

I cried out. *Mine.*

I heard the whisper in my head.

No, he's not mine. My belly clenched. But some part of me wanted him to be. I didn't just want his body or his handsome face, no, I wanted his wounded soul too.

I wanted all of him, and that scared the shit out of me.

I moved faster, desperate for release. All I had to focus on right now was the red-hot desire.

He filled me so thoroughly, I felt him everywhere.

His gaze locked on my face. Intense. Intimate.

I whimpered. "I'm close."

"Good. Give it to me, Jess. *Now*."

Then he kissed me. His finger rubbed my clit, his cock moved inside me, and his mouth claimed mine.

I screamed into his mouth and a brilliant orgasm flared along my nerve endings. I clung to him, my body shaking. North continued to pound inside me.

Then he yanked my hips down, and a low, animal sound escaped him. I felt his hot release spurt inside me.

Fighting for air, I collapsed against his shoulder.

He turned his face and nuzzled my neck. He breathed me in.

Feelings erupted inside me. I couldn't let myself fall for him. I didn't know what this was between us, but the last thing I needed was a broken heart.

"I'm glad I turned up on your doorstep," he said quietly.

I squeezed my eyes shut. I could deal with my own worries later. For now, this man needed me.

I ruffled his hair. "Me too."

"I didn't come here for this."

"I know." I pressed my mouth softly to his.

This time the kiss was gentle. His hand slid down to my hip, and I shivered. His lips curved. He obviously liked how much he affected me.

Then he rose from the stool, and I let out a squeak. I clamped my arms and legs around him. But he held me tightly and didn't let me fall.

"Not done with you yet," he said.

I licked my lips. "Okay."

He hitched his pants up and carried me down the hall.

The lamp was on in my bedroom. My bed was covered with a pretty white coverlet that I'd picked up at a store in Dawn.

North lay me on the bed. He looked at me until I wanted to squirm.

"What?" I breathed.

"Love looking at you. Love looking at you naked on your pretty bed." His lips curved. "I love knowing I'm going to fuck you in it."

One big hand slid around my ankle. His hand ran up my calf, my thigh, igniting sensations everywhere. He pressed a knee to the bed, then leaned forward and dropped a kiss to my stomach.

"I love your body."

"I'm glad," I gasped.

Then his head lowered as he pushed my thighs apart. "Let me show you how much."

CHAPTER TEN

North

God, Jess was beautiful.

The lamp cast a gold glow over her face and bare skin. We were lying in her bed, and it was late, but neither of us cared. I let my fingers drift over the freckles dotting her cheek.

I was flat on my back, and she was leaning over me, her fingers tracing over my tattoo.

"Why a dragon?" she asked.

I grinned. "I was a twenty-something kid, and thought it looked cool."

She smiled, her finger following the dragon's tail up over my shoulder.

"Now, I feel like it represents me. Out there, fighting the monsters. Keeping people safe."

"A protector." Her hand moved to my arm, touching the tattoo on my bicep. "And this?" Her fingers traced over the twin snakes wound around a winged staff.

"It's a caduceus. A pre-invasion symbol for medicine."

"So your ink is perfect for you. Representing the healer and the warrior." She kissed my chest. "It's badass, like you."

"I try."

She cupped my cheek. "And don't forget that. What you do is important. I know you blame yourself for Drew's death, but the monster took his life. You were there for him at the end. He wasn't alone."

My throat tightened. "Yeah."

"How many people have you saved since then?"

"I don't keep count."

"I'm pretty sure that Joe and Hudson are happy that you're a part of Hunter Squad." She peppered more kisses across my skin. "I know I am."

Need pulsed through me. I rolled her onto her back and pinned her to the bed. "I'm really glad you joined us, Jess."

I kissed her hungrily. She arched into me, her desperate moan echoing around us. My cock hardened. I'd already taken her twice, but I wanted her again.

I hooked my arms under her thighs, pushed them wide. Rising up, I notched my cock at her slick folds. Urgency rode me hard. I needed to be inside her. Needed it like a drug. I thrust my hips forward and slid home.

My low groan mingled with Jess' husky cry. She felt so good. So hot and tight.

"Jess—" I started moving, keeping my thrusts slow and deep.

Her dark gaze locked on mine, and I couldn't look away. I felt things... So many damn things. Things I hadn't ever wanted to feel.

"I can't get enough of you," I panted.

Her nails scratched down my back. "I love you inside me." One of her hands slid up and into my hair. She tugged hard and I loved it.

Damn. I thrust into her faster. I wasn't going to last much longer. Then my mouth was on hers, swallowing her moans.

She ripped her mouth free. Her inner muscles clenched on my cock. It was my name on her lips as she came.

I watched her face as she came, then my cock swelled. I couldn't hold back. As my orgasm hit, my spine bent. I thrust as deep as I could go, pumping her full of me.

I nearly collapsed on top of her, but had enough brainpower left to slide to the side.

She curled into me, and I nuzzled her hair. She smelled good. She felt good.

I felt good.

Being with her...made everything good.

"Mmm, a girl could get used to this."

"Not sleeping?"

She smiled. "A hot guy with a hot bod, and hot sex with hot orgasms."

I ran a thumb over her cheek. I touched each freckle one by one. Her skin was satin smooth. "Yeah, I could get used to it, too."

We both stilled, then she pushed at my chest. "I think

we need sustenance. I might have some leftover pizza." She pulled a face. "I haven't had much time to cook, and the pizza place here in Dawn is so good."

"You cook?"

"I do." She grinned. "One day, I'll make you my chicken enchiladas. With a special Ramos family enchilada sauce."

"Sounds amazing." I really liked the idea of Jess cooking for me.

"But you'll have to make do with cold pizza right now."

"Wouldn't be the first time."

She strolled out of the bedroom naked, shooting me a wide, saucy grin. I drank in every curve. I liked that she was confident in her body.

When she came back, she was holding a pizza box in one hand and a stack of napkins in the other. I sat up against the mound of pillows.

She set the box down in the center of the bed, then sat beside me and snuggled in. "I hope you like pepperoni."

"Love it."

I loved this. A warm pang hit my chest. I'd dated before, but nothing serious. I'd never wanted to lounge in bed eating pizza naked with a woman before.

Before Jess.

Shit. I was sliding too deep, too fast. Jess was here to work. I knew she didn't want to mess things up.

"North, stop thinking so hard."

I met her gaze. "You and me, it comes with complications."

"It doesn't have to. We'll sort this out." She gestured with a slice of pizza between us. "Don't overthink it."

I nodded.

"Now eat your pizza."

"Yes, boss." I took a bite out of a slice.

She made little noises as she ate. Soon, I was hard again. My cock was not getting the memo that it was late, and we'd already had more than our fill of her.

"We should get some sleep." She took the now-empty box and set it on the bedside table. Then she saw the tented sheet over my lap and cocked a brow. "Might be a little hard to sleep like that."

"Ignore it."

"That would be impossible." She pulled the sheet off me, baring my rock-hard cock. Then she crawled across the bed, smiling. "Why don't you let me help you out?"

I leaned back, my muscles tight. "Okay."

Her hand circled the base of my cock. My hips jerked.

"Just relax." She kissed my thigh. "I'll take good care of you."

Jess

AN INSISTENT BEEP WOKE ME.

I opened my eyes and realized I was lying on top of North.

He was flat on his back, and I was nestled on him like

a baby koala. One big hand was possessively cupping my ass. *Mmm*.

I didn't want to get up. I was warm, and North was a surprisingly comfy bed. Besides, it was still dark outside.

The beep came again and I realized it was my communicator.

Sighing, I rolled off him. I sensed the instant he woke. I reached for my comm unit, taking note of a few new aches in a few interesting places.

I answered the device, keeping the visual off. "Ramos."

"Jess." It was Sasha's voice. "Sorry to wake you. Emergency callout."

Shit. I glanced at my clock. It was only 2:30 in the morning. This couldn't be good. "Got it." I pushed my hair back.

"Jameson will be there to pick you up in five minutes. Okay?"

My heart kicked. Five minutes was not long enough for North to get home.

"Jess?" Sasha said.

I shook my head. "Sure thing, Sasha. I'll be ready."

There was the sound of another communicator pinging.

"You've got North." He sat up, holding his comm unit, his voice gravelly from sleep.

"Why didn't you answer the first time I called you?" Sasha said.

"I was sleeping."

"Well, wake up. We've got a job."

"What is it?"

"A group of people were taken from the town of Picton."

North cursed. "That's not far from here, right?"

"Right. It's not far from the old national park area that borders Lake Burragorang."

I assumed the national park was all bushland filled with monsters.

"They have solid walls around the town." North's brow creased. "How come people were out at nighttime?"

"They didn't go out." Sasha's voice was grim. "They were guards. Five of them were taken. A group of monsters attacked the wall."

He straightened. "Hell."

"Jameson is coming to your place to pick you up."

North glanced at me. "Um..."

I nodded.

He raised his brows. *You sure?*

I nodded again. I wasn't one to try and hide things. I'd face the consequences head on.

"I'm not at home," he said.

"Oh?" Sasha paused. "Give me your location, and I'll pass it along to Jameson. I hope you left the lucky lady happy."

He sighed. "I'm at Jess' place."

There was a long beat of silence. "Ohhhh."

"Not now, Sash. I'll catch you later."

"You sure will, North Connors."

He rose. Luckily, I'd put his clothes in the dryer earlier. As he dressed, I pulled on cargo pants and a black T-shirt.

The cat was out of the bag now. I wasn't sure how I

felt about it. Nerves skated through me. Still, I'd welcomed North to my bed. I couldn't resist him. I had to woman-up and accept the consequences.

"You okay?" His hands rested on my shoulders.

"Yes. Ready to kick some monster ass?"

"Hell yeah." He dropped a quick kiss to my lips.

As I finished tying my hair up in a ponytail, there was a flash of lights outside the front of my house. I pushed the blind aside and saw a rugged all-terrain vehicle idling on the street.

"Ready?" North asked.

I lifted my chin. "Ready." Then I remembered something. "Wait." I snatched up the small object off the bedside table where I'd set it earlier after I'd thrown his clothes in the dryer. I'd found it in his pocket. "Don't forget this."

I held up the small robot.

His hands curled around it.

"Hudson said it would keep you safe," I murmured.

He dropped a quick kiss to my lips, then slid the robot into his pocket.

We headed out the front door, and I ensured it was locked behind us. When we reached the vehicle, I saw Jameson sitting in the driver's seat. North opened the front passenger door.

Our squad leader's face was serious as he looked at us.

I slid into the back seat. "Hey."

He looked back at me, then at North. "Is this going to be a problem?"

"No," North said.

I shook my head.

"Good." Jameson looked straight ahead and set the vehicle in drive. "We're going to get Zeke and Marc next. Kai's meeting us at Squad Command."

My tense shoulders relaxed. He wasn't going to say anything else, or make a big deal of it.

The twins lived next door to each other, several streets away. They piled into the back of the vehicle with me.

"Evening," Marc said. "Or should I say morning?"

Soon, we drove out of the front gate of Dawn, waving at the guards as they closed it behind us.

"Five guards were taken from Picton?" North said.

"Yeah, sounds bad. The monsters attacked a weak spot in the wall where repairs were being done." Jameson's hands flexed on the wheel. "The security squad on duty tonight is already busy dealing with a landslide on the central coast. Besides, they're not equipped to deal with a large group of monsters like we are."

No, that was definitely Hunter Squad's domain.

We reached Squad Command and idled at the huge front gates. A moment later, the gates slowly opened. Guards waved us in, and soon Jameson drove down into the underground parking garage.

Moments later, we were in our locker room, gearing up.

I glanced at North. He was already in his armor, methodically checking his medical backpack.

I understood now why he was so careful and conscientious. All because of a young man who hadn't had the chance to live.

"All right." Jameson hefted his carbine up against his broad shoulder. "I'm not sure what we're heading into, but we have a group of monsters to deal with. I need everyone sharp." He shot a quick glance at me and North.

I lifted my chin and met his hazel gaze.

Jameson nodded. "Let's get these people back."

As we strode into the hangar, the rotors were already spinning on the quadcopter. We jogged over and climbed in the back.

"Welcome aboard," Colbie said. "Nothing like a little late-night flying."

"Let's get airborne, Colbie," Jameson said.

I strapped in, and a second later, the Talon lifted off.

CHAPTER ELEVEN

HUNTER SQUAD

North

The Talon flew through the night darkness. Everyone was quiet and tense. We knew we were heading into a shitty situation.

Five adults gone. *Shit*. A muscle ticked in my jaw.

I glanced at Jess. Her face was set, focused.

Picton was inland of Dawn. Pre-invasion, it had been a small town surrounded by hills and farms that despite its close proximity to Sydney, still had a country feel to it.

Now, Picton was a fraction of its former size. The walled township sat in the center of the ruins of the larger community.

I looked out the side window of the Talon. It was too dark to see much more than glimpses given by the Talon's flying lights. All I saw were the shadows of uninhabited buildings below.

"Picton's dead ahead," Colbie said.

I glanced forward. Through the cockpit window, I

spotted the circular walls of the town, which were all lit up. It vaguely looked like an old castle set in a wasteland of rubble.

Colbie flew over the walls, and I saw heavily-armed guards standing in one of the guard towers. They were on high alert. We landed on one of the landing pads inside.

As soon as we touched down, a group of three people strode toward us—two men and a woman.

We all climbed out of the Talon.

"I'm Jameson Steele, the leader of Hunter Squad," Jameson said, holding out a hand.

The youngest man nodded. "I'm James Pitt, the leader of Picton. This is Arabella Spencer, our head of security." The older woman nodded. "And Daniel Legge. He was on duty on the wall during the attack."

I glanced at the dark-skinned man. He was probably my age. His head was wrapped in bandages.

"Tell us what happened," Jameson asked.

Daniel swiped a shaky hand across his mouth. He still looked rattled. "Monsters attacked the west wall."

"We're doing some rehab work there and there was some scaffolding set up," Arabella added. "They'd never paid any attention to it before."

I sucked in a breath. The monsters were smart enough to aim for a weak spot.

"What kind of creatures?" Jess asked, pulling out her communicator and widening the screen. "Can you describe them?"

Daniel shook his head. "That's the thing. It was a big mob of them, but they weren't all alike. I mean, I'd seen packs of similar monsters before, but nothing like this."

"Anything you can describe about them would help," Jess said.

The man pulled in a shaky breath. "There were three different breeds. Some were big, walked on all fours, and had a long tail. Others walked on two feet, but I didn't get a good look at those ones. The third type were small and fast, jumping everywhere. I reckon they had some possum in them. Never seen anything like it before."

A cold chill skated through me. Jess blinked, then got busy taking notes.

"We managed to kill a few, but then they snatched some of the guards. They got Chris and Marina first. They killed Stefan." A spasm crossed Daniel's face. "Then they took Gus, Harry and Kitt. They retreated. Carried them away."

Shit.

"Which direction?" Jameson asked.

Daniel rubbed the side of his head. "Um, north. They went north."

"Okay, Daniel." Jameson nodded. "We're going to get your people back."

"Please." He grabbed Jameson's arm. "They're all good people."

"We'll bring them home," Marc said.

"Thank you," James said before his face crumpled. "Kitt's my wife. Our three children are asleep, and I don't know what I'm going to tell them when they wake up."

Sympathy filled me. I wanted to reassure him, but I couldn't make any promises that I couldn't keep.

Jameson nodded and turned to face us. We jogged

back to the quadcopter, and a second later, we were back in the air.

"We're heading north, Colbie." Jameson stayed standing, holding a handgrip above his head. "Sasha, I need you searching for heat signatures."

"Acknowledged," the comms officer replied. "We already have a drone in the air."

"It was a group of monsters working together. They took the guards alive, so we're working on the assumption that those humans are still breathing. Let's find them."

"I'm scanning now," Sasha said.

"You think they were taken like the two boys?" I asked Jess. "To put in cocoons?"

"Maybe." A groove formed on her forehead. "It's all so strange. These different breeds of monsters working together. To what end?" She tapped a boot on the floor. "How are they communicating?" She looked lost in thought, then tapped on her communicator again.

"I reckon maybe the cocoon thing is like a fridge to them," Marc said. "Keeps their snacks fresh until they need them."

"Gross," Zeke said.

"I have some heat signatures on screen," Sasha's excited voice filled our earpieces.

Everyone straightened.

"Did they head toward the forest?" Jess asked.

"No, they're still tracking north through the ruins of Picton. They're moving fast."

"Can you pick up the five humans?" Jameson asked.

"No, they're all too close together. The heat signatures are overlapping each other."

"What's north of here?" Jess asked.

"As far as I know, more ruins of the surrounding towns," I said.

"Nothing of interest," Sasha said. "Wait. I do see a larger, industrial building and...it looks like an orchard. Wait, yes, it's an old apple orchard. They used to manufacture cider."

"I like cider," Marc said.

"It's been abandoned for decades," Sasha said, "but..."

"Maybe the monsters are using it," Jameson said. "Keep tracking them, Sash."

"Hell." Sasha's voice was taut with tension. "Jameson, the monsters just split into two groups, dammit."

I leaned forward and dangled my hands between my legs.

"One group is continuing north," Sasha said. "The other is milling around. Dammit, I can't see where the humans are. They could be with either group."

"Why did one group stop?" Kai asked.

"They're waiting for us," Jess said.

Heads whipped around to look at her.

"What?" Kai asked.

"They know we're coming. They're waiting to stop us."

Jameson checked his carbine. "Then they're in for a nasty surprise. Hunter Squad, let's do this."

"Fuck, yeah." Marc lifted his own weapon. "Time to take down some monsters."

I met Jess' gaze and nodded. She nodded back.

Jess

"THERE THEY ARE," Colbie said from the cockpit.

I stood, and gripped an overhead hand hold, and looked out the side window.

A spotlight beam from the Talon illuminated the monsters below.

They were milling in a park bounded by an old subdivision, whose houses were now all rubble. I sucked in a breath. Smaller monsters were swarming around, interspersed with larger ones.

As we all strapped on our rappel cables, Jameson slid the side door open. We were assaulted by grunts, moans, and yowls coming from below.

"Jesus," Kai muttered.

None of us had seen monsters congregate like this. Hell, I'd seen larger monsters eat smaller ones before.

Not work together like a team.

A chaotic, bloodthirsty team.

"Let's do this," Jameson said. "Kai, man the turret and take out what you can from the air."

Kai nodded. "You got it, Jameson."

"Everyone else, let's go."

"Hell, yeah," Marc yelled.

Jameson turned and jumped. Zeke leaped right behind him.

I glanced out and watched them whizz down.

"After you," Marc said.

I jumped next. The night air was cool on my face and

my gloved hands gripped my carbine. My boots hit the ground, and I disconnected the line.

Instantly, a small monster leaped at me.

I got the impression of gray fur, huge eyes, and claws. Big claws.

I whipped my weapon up and fired.

A second later, North landed beside me. Then Marc.

Zeke and Jameson were back-to-back, their lasers lighting up the night. I stayed close to North and Marc, spraying the closest creatures.

"Fuck," North muttered.

There were so many. My throat was dry.

A larger creature, about the size of a large dog, bounded at us, its jaws snapping.

We both fired on it, then Marc joined in too. The creature went down, and Marc leaped over and kept firing.

Something hit the back of my legs and I stumbled. North spun and fired.

I turned and saw one of the gray possum-like creatures. It lay twitching on the ground, black blood oozing onto the grass.

North advanced, his carbine up and his face like stone.

I moved up beside him, firing on more monsters. The creatures darted away.

There was a loud squawk. To our left, a monster darted out of the trees in the park. It ran on two long legs and had a long neck, and sharp beak. It aimed right at North.

"North!" I yelled.

At my warning, he spun and fired. The bird-like creature was quick, darting side to side and avoiding the laser fire. I pulled my knife and waited, waited…

I tossed it. It hit the monster in the face, and it went down, squawking. North stood over it and fired. It slumped to the grass.

"What the hell was that?" I retrieved my knife and wiped it on the grass.

"Looks like it has some emu DNA in it," he said

I shoved the knife back in its sheath.

The others were fighting close by in the middle of a mob of monsters.

"Take that, you assholes," Marc yelled.

The Talon flew overhead. A large laser fired from the turret, cutting into the largest monster in the group. Its big body shuddered.

"Help me."

The faint voice made me turn. I scanned the darkness and trees.

"Please, help."

"North, do you hear that?"

"Yeah, come on. The guys have got this." He broke into a jog.

I followed. "Be careful. I don't like this."

"I don't think monsters can speak."

"Not as far as we know," I muttered. My nerves were tight. This really didn't feel right. I touched my ear. "Sasha, we hear someone calling for help. North and I are going to investigate."

"Acknowledged. Watch yourselves."

We came out on a street on the other side of the park.

There were no monsters, just mounds of rubble from destroyed buildings, and several overturned cars.

We walked cautiously down the street.

"Hello?" I called out.

"Help! I'm over here." A gruff male voice.

I spotted a shadow on the road. As we got closer, I saw that it was an older man lying on his side.

Gasping, I ran toward him, still scanning our surroundings for monsters.

The man looked like he was in his late fifties or early sixties, with gray hair and, oh God... My stomach revolted. Something had chewed on his legs, leaving them mangled.

"Hi, there." North crouched beside the man. "I'm North. This is Jess."

"Hunter Squad?" the man asked in a shaky voice.

"That's us."

"Thank God." Air shuddered out of him. "You've got to help the others."

"What's your name?" North asked, opening his backpack.

"Gus." He coughed and winced. "Fucking monster dragged me here. Attacked Kitt first. She has kids. I leaped in front of it, and it got me instead."

"So you're a hero," I said.

He looked up at me. "Just a guy." He grimaced again.

I knew that he had to be in agony.

North quickly gave him a shot with the pressure injector. "Hang in there, Gus. We're going to get you out of here."

A snarl echoed down the street.

I whipped around. Three heavy, muscular monsters prowled toward us on four legs. Their bodies were covered in armor plating, and each had a heavy tail, topped with a round ball of bone on the end, whipping around behind them.

Great. Just great.

"That's...what dragged me here," Gus said.

Dammit. It looked like they'd used Gus as bait.

"North..."

"Let's take them down fast. Gus needs medical attention." North rose, lifting his carbine. "Hold tight, Gus."

"Light those abominations up," Gus gritted out.

One of the creatures roared.

"They look like those bony dinosaurs that had a club-like tail," I said.

"Ankylosaurus."

"You were a dino geek?"

"Maybe. I thought dinosaurs were pretty cool when I was a kid."

Then the three monsters rushed at us, gathering speed, powerful bodies moving fast.

Steeling myself, I aimed my carbine.

North and I opened fire.

CHAPTER TWELVE

HUNTER SQUAD

North

These monsters were big, and, by the sound of their snarls, very aggressive. One's gaze locked on me, burning hot. Oh, yes, it wanted to tear me to pieces and feed.

I stepped away from Gus. I didn't want him trampled.

Two of the creatures ran at me, and the other one at Jess. I heard her carbine fire.

I ran, then dodged around an overturned car.

One of the monsters crashed into the vehicle, knocking it aside, metal screeching on the ground.

Shit. They hit like a bulldozer. I fired behind me, aiming for the red glow of its eyes. Its skin was too dense to pierce. The damn things were covered in armor plating.

The second creature barreled toward me. It jumped, then swung its tail at me.

I dropped and rolled under it. The tail slammed into the car with a crunch of metal.

That tail was powerful. One hit, and I'd be a mess of broken bones.

I jumped onto one of the cars, firing down at the pair of monsters. Snarls and growls filled the air. I yanked a grenade off my belt, then tossed it as I leaped off the car.

Boom.

I looked over my shoulder. One monster was down, moving weakly.

The other swiveled and ran straight at me.

Shit.

There was another car in front of me. A van. Its side door was open.

I dove inside, and scrambled through the back of the vehicle.

Bang.

The monster hit the van like a bomb blast and the side crumpled in. I slid out the back door.

The monster rounded the van and roared at me.

I yanked my knife out of the sheath on my thigh, and jammed it into the monster's eye. It howled.

Where was Jess? Dodging the snarling creature while it was preoccupied, I sprinted into the street. I spotted her, still firing on her monster.

I ran over, then heard noises behind me. In the distance, my creature was shaking its head, my knife still stuck in its eye.

I reached Jess and we pressed our backs together.

"One down," I told her. "And one very unhappy."

"Their skin is too hard," she fired again. "But their underbelly is soft."

Great. I didn't really want to get under one of these.

"Distract my monster," she said.

Right. I ran to the side, and waved my arms. Jess' monster turned to face me, its red eyes locking on me.

That's it. I had no idea what she was planning, but I trusted her.

The monster stalked toward me, its powerful body creeping closer. I raised my carbine and opened fire. Laser hit the armor plating with no effect. It still kept coming.

I backed up.

A snarl came from behind me and I looked over my shoulder. My monster was perched on a car, watching me with a hungry gaze from its uninjured eye.

My heart kicked. "Whatever you have planned, Jess, now's the time."

The first monster leaped into the air at me.

At that moment, Jess sprinted in from the side, sliding feet first on the ground like a baseball player into home base.

She fired up at the monster.

I had a clear view of the softer, yellow underbelly. The laser fire ripped into it.

The monster went down like a ton of bricks.

Jess just managed to roll away and get to her feet. She snatched a grenade off her belt and swiveled.

The monster behind me roared, it's fang-filled mouth open. It was two meters away, powerful body getting ready to pounce.

Without missing a beat, Jess tossed the grenade—right into the beast's mouth.

As it jumped, I backed up, firing at its belly.

Boom.

It jerked, and I ducked. Gore splattered the side of my armor.

Looking up, I grinned at Jess.

She grinned back.

Then I heard a low groan.

Gus.

My smile fled as I raced over to the injured man.

"Cover me," I said.

Jess nodded.

I dropped down beside Gus and pulled my backpack closer. "How are you doing, Gus?"

"Better. Doesn't hurt now. Whatever you gave me did the trick."

My heart squeezed. His legs were mangled, and the shot I'd given him wouldn't dull all of the pain. The fact that he wasn't feeling anything wasn't a good sign.

"Hang in there." I got busy applying tourniquets to his thighs and touched my ear. "Jameson, I have an injured man in his late fifties. He needs an emergency evac once the area is clear."

"Acknowledged. Colbie is on standby." I heard the sound of carbine fire both in the distance, and across the comm line.

"I'm ready whenever it's safe to land," Colbie said. "I can do a hot evac if required."

"Gus, we need to get you stabilized, then get you out of here."

The older man gripped my arm. "The monsters took the others. Carried them off."

"We'll find them."

"Please. They're good people." Blood splattered on his lips.

No. "Just stay calm."

"Those people are my family. Lost my wife and kids in the invasion. All these people kept me together, gave me a reason to go on. Promise me you'll find them." His voice was getting fainter.

I took his hand. "I promise you." I knew I shouldn't, but I couldn't let this man down. "Hunter Squad never leaves anyone behind. We'll bring them home."

"Thanks." He relaxed, a smile on his face.

Dammit, I gave him another injection. My chest was so tight I could barely breathe. I put more pressure on his wounds. "Stay with me, Gus."

He looked up, his face free of stress and pain. "I can see my Clair. And my boys. Missed them so much."

"Gus—"

He squeezed my hand. "Thanks, North. I didn't want to be alone in the dark."

I squeezed back and felt him take his last breath.

Be at peace, Gus. A mix of emotions rioted through me.

I couldn't save him, but I was glad that he'd found peace. The old memories reared up, threatening to choke me.

Then a hand touched my shoulder.

"You're not alone in the dark either," Jess murmured. "Good job giving him what he needed."

I managed a nod, then touched my ear. "Colbie, cancel the evac."

"Sorry, North," the pilot murmured.

A moment later, Jameson and the others appeared. Jameson looked at Gus and his jaw tightened.

"I'll help you bag his body," Kai said.

"Then we continue on." I rose. "The others were carried away and could still be alive."

And I had promised Gus that I'd bring them home.

Jess

WE REACHED the edge of the orchard.

Apple trees stretched away into the darkness, as far as we could see. The neatly planted rows cast deep shadows, offering perfect places to hide.

In the distance, lay the dark bulk of a large warehouse building. It was where they'd made the cider. Sasha said that it had once had a restaurant and cellar.

It was easy to imagine families escaping from the city on the weekend, eating at the restaurant and sipping cider, while their kids ran through the trees.

Before. Before the aliens and before the monsters.

I glanced at North beside me.

He'd been quiet since we'd loaded Gus' body onto the Talon.

God, how hard was it to treat people and still lose them? Just being there had been tough for me, and I knew it was worse for North because he felt it was his job to save his patients.

And I knew he'd be thinking of Drew.

I nudged him. "Okay?"

He looked down at me. "Yeah. Gus was badly hurt. He would've lost his legs and... I was glad we were there."

"He was too."

North straightened. "Now, let's find his friends and bring them home."

"We will."

Jameson waved a hand and we crept quietly through the orchard, nerves tight and everyone on full alert.

"There are no heat signatures showing in the trees," Sasha said. "But there are several in the shed."

I knew that some monsters ran cooler and didn't always show up on scans. I eyed the dark trees around us. I stepped forward, my boot hitting some old, rotting apples on the ground. I kicked one aside.

"Everyone stay sharp," Jameson murmured. "I've got a bad feeling."

Clutching my carbine, I moved closer toward the warehouse. It looked like it had been constructed out of sheet metal, and was still in pretty good condition. There was damage at one end, and a tree was growing out of the roof, but the rest of it looked intact.

A squawking sound punctured the silence. All of us whipped our weapons up.

"What was that?" Marc whispered.

Another squawk.

Above us.

A dark shadow sprang from an apple tree and hit me. It knocked me to the ground.

Flapping wings beat at my face and chest, and a beak stabbed into my armor. *Hell.*

North appeared and kicked the monster off me. He reached down and hauled me up.

I spun and saw the creature hopping on the ground. It was sort of bird-like, with black, ragged wings, and it was the size of a small dog. It had a long, sharp beak, and red eyes.

More of the creatures poured out of the trees. Laser fire lit up the orchard.

North and I fired on the monsters.

Another monster leaped on my back, pulling at my hair. I spun and knocked it away.

There was rustling in the tree, and I aimed up.

A huge bird monster took flight. I felt sharp claws grip my armor at the back of my neck, and then I was lifted off my feet.

"North!" I fired at the monster, kicking my feet. The creature jerked, still flapping its wings furiously.

Hands gripped my boots and yanked me down.

The monster let me go and I fell back against North.

"Are you okay, Jess? Are you hurt?"

My pulse was racing, but otherwise I was fine. "I'm all right."

Suddenly, all the creatures stopped attacking us. Some landed on branches, and a few settled on the ground. They froze. The one right in front of us cocked its head like... It was listening to something. Then they all took flight. I glanced up and watched the black shadows flapping into the night sky. They disappeared from view into the inky darkness.

"What the fuck?" Marc scowled. "Where did they go?"

"Just be glad they're gone," Jameson said.

"We've lost the element of surprise," Kai murmured, glancing at the warehouse.

I frowned, then clicked on the light on my shoulder. "Guys, I've got prints on the ground. Human and monster."

"Our missing guards?" Jameson asked.

"I hope so."

"Doesn't matter if the monsters know we're coming, we're *not* leaving those people." He touched his ear. "Sasha, we need backup."

"On it. I'm not sure who's available, or what their ETA will be."

"We'll manage until then. We'll wait—"

There was a loud screech. It came from the warehouse.

"Help! God, someone help us." A faint voice. "*Please*." Then it turned into a wail of terror.

"Oh, God." Goosebumps formed on my skin.

"Scratch that," Jameson said. "We're going in."

"Jameson, wait," Sasha said. "There are multiple heat signatures. You'll be severely outnumbered."

"Someone needs help now. If we wait, they're dead." He looked at us. "Who's with me?"

Zeke snorted. "Dumb question."

"Hell, yeah," Marc said.

Kai nodded, then North.

I lifted my chin. "Let's do this."

We stayed in a tight group, moving toward the building. We all had our weapons up.

The large sliding door on the side of the warehouse was open. An old, rusted tractor sat outside.

The inside of the building was stygian darkness.

Jameson cursed. "We can't see a thing." He released a breath. "Flashlights on."

We all clicked on our lights. The beams barely penetrated the dark.

We moved inside.

My heartbeat thudded heavily in my ears. Then I saw...something.

I walked closer, gasped. "Guys."

I reached out and touched the sticky weblike substance that we'd seen in the cave where we'd rescued Hudson. It was everywhere, crisscrossing the space, covering boxes, running up the walls.

Marc stepped on some, then kicked it off. "It's sticky as hell."

"Help! Is someone there? *Please*."

The male voice echoed from deeper in the building. We cautiously moved forward. We couldn't risk calling out. There were monsters here.

"Oh, fuck," Jameson breathed.

He was in front, and his flashlight illuminated cocoons. Lots of them. My gut curdled.

"This looks like a really bad horror movie," Marc whispered.

They couldn't all have humans in them? Surely.

A cocoon closest to us started moving, the sticky substance stretching.

Jameson pulled out his combat knife and sliced it open.

A dog fell out. Its fur was matted and it started barking wildly. It got to its feet, then shot off like a bullet.

"Fuck me," Marc said.

Another cocoon started moving. We walked closer. My heartbeat echoed in my ears.

There was a sound behind me, and I turned. "North?"

I frowned. He wasn't there. He'd been standing right behind me.

"North?"

Where did he go?

"Hunter Squad." Sasha's tense voice. "Heat signatures are lighting up all around you. Get out!"

What? My gut contracted.

Then a long, deafening roar echoed through the building.

CHAPTER THIRTEEN

North

I stared at the cocoons, my gut tightened.

There were so damn many.

There was a noise in the shadows behind me and I swiveled, gun aimed.

I didn't see anything. Just more of those damn cocoons. I peered into the darkness but didn't see anything.

My senses tingled. Something was there.

I shook my head. The sooner we got out of here, the better.

I turned back to look at the squad. Jameson pulled a knife.

Suddenly, something grabbed me from behind and yanked me backward.

Something strong.

A dark, wiry arm covered my face, muffling my shout.

I hammered against my attacker, and it dragged me back into the darkness, away from the others.

"Hunter Squad," Sasha said. "Heat signatures are lighting up all around you. Get out!"

I heard carbine fire as I struggled. I caught glimpses of my squad mates fighting. A giant monster bounded toward Marc and Zeke. Jess fired on several small, agile creatures. Hell, they didn't even know I was gone.

The monster holding me dragged me across the warehouse. I kicked and jerked, but it held me firmly. It was so damn strong. Its hold loosened for a second, then it slammed me to the ground. The air rushed out of me.

A clawed hand in the center of my back kept me pinned to the dirty concrete.

I looked up.

My heart kicked my ribs. There were two of them. They were the same creatures we'd seen in the cave where we'd rescued Hudson.

Their skin was ink black, and their long, skinny bodies were all lean, honed muscle. Long arms were tipped with big claws. One hauled me off the ground, holding me in the air, my feet dangling. Then it reached up and plucked the earpiece from my ear.

Fuck. I fumbled for my knife. I could still hear my squad fighting. Snarls and growls filled the warehouse.

"Come on...assholes," I gritted out. My hand curled around the hilt of my combat knife.

Then the creature holding me rammed me against the wall. I moved my hand and jammed my knife into its gut.

It let out a hissing noise, and the claws at my throat tightened until I couldn't breathe. I felt blood trickle down my neck. I tried to kick the thing. It yanked the knife out of its side, and didn't seem affected.

The knife clattered to the ground. The second monster stepped closer. There were no eyes, but it seemed to be focused on my face. It cocked its head.

"Come...on. Fight me."

The hold on my neck loosened and I sucked in air. I filled my burning lungs.

Then the second monster made a noise.

Its snout flared open. *What the fuck?* Horror froze me. I stared at the strange, small sucker mouth inside.

Then, a sticky substance shot out and sprayed onto my face.

Fuck me. I turned my head and clamped my mouth closed. The sticky web stuck to my face and body. I twisted, trying to get free, but a moment later, I was stuck to the wall.

The first monster stepped back. I kept struggling, but I was stuck in place by the substance.

"*Argh.*" I shoved against the stuff. I could still hear my squad in the distance. I had to get their attention. They'd come for me.

But the roars and grunts of monsters filled the air.

My thoughts turned to Jess.

God. I hadn't been looking for her. I didn't want to have feelings for someone. Not these strong emotions. It hurt to lose someone and I didn't want to lose her.

I was falling for her, and now, I wish I hadn't been

afraid. I wished I'd grabbed ahold of her and never let go. I wished I'd told her how I felt.

Not giving up. I kept struggling. I didn't want to die like this. I sure as hell didn't want to end up as a mummified body in a cocoon.

My squad needed me.

I needed Jess.

More sticky web hit my face. The stuff bound around me until I could barely move.

Soon, I'd be locked in a cocoon.

No. I kept struggling, but more of the substance covered my face until I couldn't see anymore.

No.

Jess

THE MONSTERS CAME at us from all directions.

There were lots of the small, possum-like ones that scuttled across the floor and sprung into the air.

I fired on them.

One of the large monsters with a long tail and armor plating leaped at the twins. All the squad were fighting and firing their weapons.

"Take that, you scaly bastard." Marc's voice.

Zeke and Marc were working together. Zeke leaped onto the monster, as Marc ducked under the swinging tail. Zeke slapped an explosive charge onto the creature's neck, then jumped off and rolled.

The charge went off, and gore and scales flew in all directions.

Jameson and Kai were firing on more bird-like monsters that were fluttering on the ceiling. They had their carbines up, swiveling to take each shot.

But the monsters kept coming.

Nearby, a cocoon started shaking.

"Help! Get me out." It was a panicked female voice.

I kept firing on the possum monsters.

A large cat-like creature raced out of the darkness and pounced at me. I hit the ground, rolled and fired. With a snarl, it dropped to the floor.

"Fire in the hole," Kai yelled.

I heard the sound of metal pinging on the ground.

Boom.

The grenade exploded. I ducked, and threw my arms over my head. I saw several monsters fly through the air.

I stayed down, then ran toward the cocoon. "Hold on, I'm here to help."

"Thank God," came the muffled voice inside. "Please, get me out."

I was reaching for my knife when another armored Ankylosaurus-monster skulked out of the darkness. Its heavy tail moved side to side behind it. I whipped my carbine up and fired at its eyes.

The creature's roar was deafening. Yeah, yeah, you're big and scary. Now, jump and show me your belly.

It leaped.

I pulled the trigger, aiming for its weak spot.

Its body jerked and it fell, landing on its side. I waited a beat, but it didn't get up and no more monsters appeared. I prayed that we were starting to thin them out.

Zeke appeared beside me. "Okay?"

"Cover me," I told him. "I found one of the guards."

The quiet man nodded.

I yanked out my knife and started hacking into the cocoon. I gritted my teeth, sawing through the substance. "Hang on."

"Jess," Zeke said sharply.

I looked up. There was a creature, hidden by the shadows, and I could just see red eyes glowing in the darkness.

Shit. I gripped my carbine. The hairs on the back of my neck rose. It was tall and I thought I got the impression of wings, but I could be imagining. I felt...a sense of intelligence and menace.

Then the eyes blinked out. Nothing.

"Where did it go?"

"I'll check. You help her." Zeke strode forward.

I resumed cutting into the cocoon and finally I freed the woman's head.

"Thank you." She had matted blonde hair and was covered in sticky goop. She spat to the side and then started coughing.

"Take it easy." I helped her out. "Are you Kitt?"

She blinked. "Yes."

"We're Hunter Squad."

There was relief on her face.

"I've got another one," Marc yelled.

I glanced over and saw him cutting into a cocoon. He freed a sobbing man.

I helped Kitt free of the cocoon and she stumbled, trying to catch her balance. Then she saw the other man.

"Harry." She ran over to hug him.

"Open all the cocoons," Jameson barked.

I cut into the next cocoon. A kangaroo fell out. It was dead.

The next one was a short, stocky man. He slid to the ground, deathly still. He wasn't breathing.

"Chris!" Kitt cried.

"Where's North?" Jameson dropped down beside the man.

My chest hitched. Where was North? I hadn't seen him in the fight. "He was behind me earlier."

"I didn't see him during the fight," Kai said.

Oh God. Where was he?

Jameson started CPR on the man. Finally, he shook his head. "He's gone."

Kitt stifled a sob.

"Marina." Harry said. "And Gus. We have to find them."

God, we'd have to tell them about Gus.

"Everyone keep checking the cocoons." Jameson touched his ear. "North, respond. North?"

Panicked flutters filled me. Where was he? He wouldn't just leave.

Not of his own accord.

A crushing sensation hit me. I couldn't lose him.

I'd lost my mother. I'd lost my father. I had a big extended family, but I'd lost the people who were mine. Who cared most about me.

I couldn't lose North.

When he looked at me, he saw me. He wanted me in a way no one ever had before. He was mine. I felt that deep in my heart.

Jameson gripped my shoulder. "We'll find him. North is the most resourceful person I know."

I nodded.

"Marina?" Kitt yelled. "Marina?"

I heard a vague noise. Pushing down the sharp-edged panic inside me, I hurried over to another cocoon and cut it open.

The woman came out coughing. She was older, her dark hair stuck to her head. Her eyes were wide and freaked out.

"Marina?" I asked. "You're safe now."

She held up a hand, clearly focused on not falling apart. "I'm... all right."

The others arrived to help pull her out.

I scanned around for North, my worry growing.

"North?" I yelled.

"There was another guard with us," Kitt said. "Gus."

I sucked in a breath. "Kitt, I'm sorry, he didn't make it."

She pressed a hand to her mouth. "No."

"I'm sorry. We were there with him at the end. He wasn't alone."

Then I spotted something in the darkness, on the ground. It was white with blue on it.

Frowning, I walked over. Then I saw what it was.

My pulse went crazy. "Jameson!"

I snatched up the small robot. "North had this. Hudson gave it to him." I spun. "North!"

We all started shouting.

"North!"

I turned and that's when I saw the carbine on the ground. Just beyond it, was a cocoon on the far wall. It was large and still wet. Freshly made.

I saw it move weakly.

My heart lodged in my throat. "North!" I ran.

CHAPTER FOURTEEN

North

I gasped for air.

It was hard to breathe.

Fuck. My face was covered entirely by the sticky substance. I couldn't see a thing. Every breath was hard work.

I dragged in another one, my lungs burning.

Wooziness made my limbs heavy. It couldn't be lack of oxygen affecting me yet. Maybe it was the damn sedative Jess' tests had detected.

Soon, I'd pass out. Jess' face filled my mind. So beautiful, tough, strong.

In such a short time, she'd made me feel so much. I felt like she'd woken me up. I hadn't realized how much I'd held myself back. I hadn't wanted to risk falling in love with someone, in case I lost them. I knew up close and personal how dangerous life could be.

Then I thought of my parents. The love they shared. All our big extended family of friends.

So much love and hope.

It was what had kept humans fighting against the aliens, against overwhelming odds.

Jess was worth the risk. She was worth everything.

I heard muffled sounds, but my brain floated away. I couldn't focus.

Don't give up. I shoved against the cocoon. I'd give anything to see Jess and my friends again.

Suddenly, light speared into my eyes.

I blinked, my vision blurry. A flashlight was shining in my face.

"North, oh God."

Jess' face filled my vision, for real. Her mouth was bracketed by tense lines. She had a knife in her hand, hacking at the cocoon.

Then Jameson was there, tearing the stuff away.

I dragged in a deep breath. Sweet air filled my lungs.

The sticky substance gave way and my body tipped forward. Jameson and Zeke caught me and lowered me to the ground.

"Just breathe." Jameson pressed fingers to the side of my neck.

I managed another breath, and the wooziness started to clear. Jess was right there, her hand cupping my cheek

"Monster...dragged me off," I rasped out.

"Take it easy." Emotion filled her gaze. "God, I was so worried."

"I'm okay. Help me sit up."

They helped me up. In front of me, I saw three people huddled together.

"We found the guards," Jess said. "One was dead." She rubbed a hand over my back.

I glanced at the remains of the cocoon and shuddered. "It was two of those creatures we saw in the cave. They spray out the sticky substance."

"Hell," Jameson growled.

"Yeah, I don't recommend it."

Jess gripped my arm. "You're okay."

I let my gaze trace over her face. "Yeah, I am now."

"How about we get the hell out of here," Jameson said.

I nodded. "Sounds good. I'm fine to move."

Jess grabbed my hand, and I let her help me up. I was feeling steadier with every second.

Kai stepped forward and held out my carbine. "I think this belongs to you."

"Thanks, Kai."

Jess stepped in front of me. "You sure you're okay?"

"Yeah."

"You worried the hell out of me."

"Sorry." I couldn't stop myself. I smoothed some of her hair back from her face. "I was worried there for a bit too." I lowered my voice. "Thinking of you kept me steady."

She looked at me, her face softening. She cupped both my cheeks, then went up on her toes and kissed me.

And everything felt better. With a low groan, I slid my arm around her waist, pulled her close, and kissed her back.

Marc hooted. "Well, well, you two are sneaky."

I ignored my friend and finished kissing my woman. I reluctantly set her down.

"Don't do that again," she said.

"Kiss you or get trapped in a monster cocoon? Can't say that second one is high on my to do list."

"Get hurt and worry me."

"Okay." I pressed another quick kiss to her lips and nuzzled her.

"I've got something that belongs to you too," she said.

I smiled. "You."

Her lips twitched. "Apart from that." She held up a small white object.

I saw the small robot and my smile widened.

"It helped me find you. We had no idea where you were or what had happened, then I saw this."

"Hudson was right, it did help protect me."

"Make sure you keep it on you all the time."

"I will." I slid the toy into my pocket.

"All right, everyone, let's get out of here," Jameson ordered.

Dodging torn cocoons and dead monsters, we stepped outside. The faint inklings of sunrise were coloring the eastern horizon in faint gold and pink.

"It's a shame we didn't find some cider," Marc said.

"I did," Zeke said. "There are some barrels inside."

"What? You didn't mention it. You should've grabbed a couple."

"Was kinda busy fighting monsters."

"Ah, guys," Sasha said. "I'm picking up something

inside the warehouse. A large heat signature is flickering in there."

Jameson frowned. "There were no monsters left."

"Something is lighting up my scans. I —"

There was a deafening roar. We spun, just in time to see the roof ripped off the warehouse. Dirt sprayed into the air.

A giant black leg broke through the top of the warehouse. Then another.

"It came out of the damn ground," Kai said.

The giant monster hauled itself out of the ruined building.

"Fuck me," Marc breathed.

"Oh, god, we're going to die," Marina whimpered.

We pushed the guards back behind us and whipped our carbines up.

"We need weapons," Kitt said urgently. "We can fight."

"Give them blasters," Jameson said, not taking his eyes off the monster.

"Oh no," Jess murmured beside me.

My head whipped up. That's when I saw the glow on the spiderlike creature's bulbous abdomen.

A sickly green-yellow.

"It's the same acid substance from the monsters on the beach," Jess said.

"Back up," Jameson bellowed. "Into the trees.

We walked backward, but the creature had locked on us and stepped forward. It had giant mandible pincers that snapped together angrily. Several red eyes locked on us.

"Light it up," Jameson said.

We opened fire. The monster roared, but looked unaffected. It stabbed at us with one leg.

Jess leaped backward, knocking into me. We hit the ground and rolled. The sharp end of the leg speared into the dirt a meter away from us.

Shit. My pulse took off like a rocket. Another leg slammed down, dirt spraying us.

"Up." I boosted her to her feet and leaped up. I yanked my knife out and stabbed at the leg.

My blade screeched across the leg. It was made of a hard black shell, impenetrable.

"The body's too hard," I yelled.

Another leg slammed down.

I dashed backward. The others were still firing but the laser wasn't doing anything.

Nearby, Zeke climbed into a tree. He moved up the branches quickly. Balanced on a thick branch, he pulled out a knife. It was far bigger than standard combat issue ones we all carried.

"Keep it busy," Zeke called out.

Marc stepped into view and waved his arms. "Hey, ugly."

It skittered around, looking at Marc and ignoring Zeke. One leg slammed down and Marc dodged.

He laughed. "Have to be quicker than that."

I saw another leg swing at him. "Marc, look out!"

He glanced back but there was nothing he could do. It swept him off his feet and tossed him into the air. He smashed into a tree trunk, then fell to the ground. With a groan, he staggered to his feet.

Above, Zeke leaped from the branch onto the creature.

He landed on one leg and clung with one arm. With his other, he lifted his knife, then hacked into the leg joint.

The creature roared. It spun, but Zeke held on. He hacked again, and again, and the leg joint broke. The creature bucked, and Zeke went flying.

"Zeke!" Marc yelled.

Zeke hit the ground hard. He tried to push up, but collapsed.

We kept firing our carbines.

Even with its broken leg, the monster hobbled closer to Zeke. *Crap.* It was going to trample him.

I raced toward my friend, firing at the monster.

But the laser fire was just making it angry.

It waved two legs in the air and let out a deafening screech.

Jess

GOD, it was huge.

We all kept firing, for all the good it was doing.

My gaze swung to North. He'd pulled a dazed Zeke up and had an arm around his broad form.

The monster let out another screech, shifting to focus on the men.

Shit, it was going to attack them.

"Hey!" I yelled and fired at its face. "Over here,

asshole."

It roared, two legs slamming down into the ground.

"North, hurry!" I shouted.

But the massive body moved, the hungry red gaze locking on North and Zeke again.

My chest locked. *No.*

There was a whoosh of sound. A Talon flew overhead, its auto-turret firing.

"Everyone get clear," Colbie's voice said across the comm line.

"Nice timing, lark," Marc said.

I raced toward North and Zeke. I slid my arm around Zeke and helped North carry his weight. Zeke looked at me, but his pupils were dilated, his face dazed.

"Concussion?" I said.

"Likely," North replied.

Suddenly, the monster reared up in front of us, one black leg spearing into the air.

It hit the Talon.

"Colbie!" Marc yelled.

The Talon spun. I gasped, my insides freezing. I imagined Colbie fighting for control.

"Hell," North said.

We watched the spinning quadcopter. It was going to crash.

But a second before it hit the trees, the aircraft evened out.

"I've got it," Colbie said. "I'm okay." The Talon moved away from the monster.

Nearby, I saw Marc's chin drop to his chest as he sucked in a breath. "Shit, lark, don't worry us like that."

"I have a warning light. I need to land." The Talon passed overhead and out of view.

The monster roared.

"Retreat," Jameson ordered.

We all turned and ran through the orchard. But Zeke couldn't move very fast, and he was heavy.

The guards ran ahead of us.

I heard crashing behind us and glanced back.

The monster was mowing through the orchard, trampling and ripping up trees.

"Faster," I cried out.

Jameson and Kai stopped, firing back on the monster. They both tossed grenades.

I heard the explosions, but it barely slowed the creature down. The monster roared again. It was gaining on us.

"Shit." Jameson glanced around.

There was nowhere to go. No shelter. No way to hide.

My throat tightened.

I looked up and met North's gaze.

I wanted to fall in love with him. I wanted to live, I wanted a life with this man.

"You guys need a little help?" a gravelly voice said over the comm.

A second Talon came into view.

Two men stood in the open doorway.

My chest hitched. It was Marcus Steele and Uncle Cruz.

Both men fired carbines down on the monster. A second later, the Talon swung around, and the large turret on the quadcopter opened fire.

"Get clear, everyone," Sasha said. "*Now*."

We kept hobbling out of the orchard. Marcus and Cruz rained down hell on the beast. Heavy laser fire ripped into the monster.

Its enraged roar turned to pained screeches.

Then, the laser fire hit the poison on the creature's back.

"Fuck," Cruz said. "*Dios mio*."

Green-yellow goo exploded into the air, then rained down.

We were out of range. The goo splattered over the monster.

The creature jerked and spun, its hard shell burning. I heard the sizzling from where we stood.

A moment later, the creature collapsed.

"Take that, you ugly fucker," Marc said, blowing out a breath.

Kai and Jameson gave each other a fist bump.

Behind Zeke's back, I felt North's fingers reach out and touch me.

"You guys do this for a living?" Kitt's face was pale.

"Not always this…" Jameson shook his head. "Yes, it's pretty much always like this. We do it because someone has to."

Kitt nodded. "Thank you. For doing that and for coming for us."

Behind Kitt, Marina and Harry both nodded.

"Always," Jameson said. "Working together is how we stay strong. It keeps us safe." He jerked his head. "Now, let's get you guys home."

We walked out of the orchard and onto a road. I saw Colbie's Talon nearby. The pilot was out, circling the quadcopter and checking the damage.

"Let's sit Zeke down," North said. "I need to check him."

We lowered Zeke to the ground. North crouched in front of the man and pulled his medical backpack off.

A second later, the other Talon came in to land, air washing over us.

Marcus and Cruz leaped out of the quadcopter and walked over to us. They were both wearing older-style, battered armor. They were both also smiling.

"We've still got it," Cruz said.

"Hell, yeah," Marcus replied.

"Good timing, Dad." Jameson and his father slapped each other on the back.

Cruz came to me and hugged me. "You okay?"

"Yes." I glanced back at the ruined warehouse in the distance. "I do want to get some more samples of the cocoons and compare them with the earlier ones."

He shook his head. "I dramatically save the day, and all you can think about is studying the monsters."

I grinned at him. "Yes, but thanks."

"You can make me your enchiladas as a thank you."

"You bet."

North flashed a small light in Zeke's eye, then pressed an injector to his neck. "He'll be fine. He just needs to be monitored."

"Luckily you've got a hard head, bro," Marc said.

Zeke just grunted.

Colbie headed over. "I missed the party."

Marc stepped toward the pilot, then stopped. "You okay, lark?"

She wagged a finger at him. "Don't call me that. I'm fine."

"You nearly crashed."

She tossed her red hair back. "Nearly doesn't count."

That's when another man emerged from the second Talon, wearing a flight suit. Colbie's face lit up. "Dad."

Finn Erickson had a tall, lean body and tousled blond hair. He caught Colbie, hauling her off her feet, and hugged her. "You okay?"

She nodded. "My Talon's fine, it'll just need minor repairs. Nice flying."

Finn smiled. "Right back at you, flygirl."

That's when North grabbed me. I grinned at him. "We made it."

He didn't reply. He just hauled me close and kissed the hell out of me.

With a moan, I gripped the front of his armor and kissed him back.

"Wait a second." Cruz frowned. "You two are…? This is kind of sudden."

I leaned into North. "Oh? How long was it until you had Aunt Santha pregnant?"

Cruz scratched the back of his neck. "This isn't about me and your aunt. It's about making sure no one takes advantage of you. About keeping you—"

"Don't worry, Uncle Cruz, this is the real deal." North looked at me and my heart melted. "Jess is mine. I promise I'll take good care of her." His thumb rubbed across my cheekbone.

"As long as I get to take care of you in return," I murmured.

"Deal."

CHAPTER FIFTEEN

HUNTER SQUAD

North

I couldn't stop looking at her.

Sunlight streamed in through the windows. After we'd safely dropped the survivors back to Picton early this morning—and watched Kitt's reunion with her husband and children—we'd returned to Squad Command.

We'd had a short debrief, stored all the cocoon samples that Jess had taken in the lab, then washed the monster crud off. Once we'd gotten to Jess' place we'd collapsed into bed.

I'd had a solid six hours of sleep.

This afternoon, we had a longer meeting scheduled with the generals to discuss a situation. But right now, all I wanted to do was look at my woman.

She was sprawled on her stomach, her dark hair loose. I leaned over and kissed her spine. She was naked and I liked that. A lot.

She was *mine*. I felt that in my soul.

A part of me was still afraid to fall in love with her all the way. To care so much when she could be snatched away.

But we couldn't live like that. Drew wouldn't have wanted that. The young man who'd been saving to buy his girlfriend a gift would've wanted everyone to not hold back, to live, to love.

I peppered kisses over Jess' skin, and she stirred and stretched.

"Mmm." Her voice was husky from sleep. "That's a nice way to wake up."

I moved back down that enticing body, letting my lips caress her skin, and pushed the sheet lower.

My cock was hard. I needed her.

I slid a hand over her smooth ass, then delved between her thighs. She moaned and lifted her hips. I pushed two fingers inside her slick warmth.

"*North...*" A throaty moan.

Need filled the word. I pulled back, then worked my fingers back inside her.

"*Yes.*" She writhed against the sheets. "I want you."

"I want you too. More than anything." I pulled her up on her knees and slid behind her. Circling my cock, I gave it a rough pump, then notched it in place between her legs. Then I thrust home.

She made a hungry sound, pushing back into me. I leaned over her and bit her shoulder. "That sound you make drives me crazy."

"Good." Her voice was breathy.

My hands locked on her hips. I pumped inside her.

"I love this," Jess breathed. "I love when you're inside me."

Whatever control I had evaporated. I reached under her body and found her clit. I kept up my heavy thrusts, and her head tipped back. I felt her inner muscles clenching on me. I looked down at her sweet ass and the way my cock was embedded inside her.

Pure possession filled me.

"North, *please*."

I pulled out, then slammed back in. I rubbed her clit harder.

"*Yes*." The sounds she made urged me on.

I was inside Jess.

I was about to come inside her.

This was where I was supposed to be. I pounded into her, then she cried out. Her pussy clamped down my cock.

I gritted my teeth, holding on. Her body shook as she came, and I felt my own release building. It was big—gathering in my gut and balls.

She looked back over her shoulder. The look in her eyes...

I couldn't hold back any longer. I rammed forward, as deep as I could go. A ragged sound ripped out of me as I came.

For a second, everything went white. All I could do was hold on and feel. Feel everything inside me from this woman. This woman who I knew was meant for me.

When reality clicked back in, I was breathing heavily and lying on the bed. Jess was tucked up against me.

"Hi," she whispered.

"Hi." I stroked my fingers through her hair.

"Did you sleep okay?" she asked.

"I think so. I can't remember anything before coming inside your sweet body."

Her slow smile warmed everything inside me.

We'd made it. We'd fought the monsters, we'd saved some people, lost some people, but we'd survived.

We'd fight again. We'd never give up. Yes, there was always a risk that we could lose the ones we loved, but loving them, every precious second spent with them, was worth it.

I understood my parents better now. They were so committed to each other. I'd seen how in love they were. Now, I knew how they felt.

"Move in with me?"

Jess blinked. "Really?" Her hand pressed against my chest, tracing over my ink.

I nodded. "I want to be with you. I want to live together, make memories together. I want to fight beside you, watch you work. I want us to be together."

She cupped my cheek. "That sounds like a good deal."

"I felt the click from the moment I first saw you. I fought it."

"I hadn't noticed." Her tone was dry. Her fingers scratched over my stubble. "I understand, North. Loving someone is a risk. You open yourself up. I lost my mom, then my dad, but I wouldn't ever give up the moments I had with them. And I want all the moments with you."

"I'm going to love you, Jessica Ramos. If you let me. You'll be mine, and I'll be yours."

The look on her face made my chest fill with warmth.

"That sounds like a really good deal," she murmured. "I accept. And yes, I'll move in with you."

Feeling so fucking happy, I lowered my head and kissed my woman.

Jess

I CIRCLED THE LAB BENCH, staring at the full, intact cocoon.

We'd collected samples from the orchard and warehouse, and managed to transport this cocoon intact. We were running a battery of new tests on it.

The x-rays showed that there was a kangaroo inside. The animal was still alive.

Curiosity and excitement sparked inside me. We had to discover what the cocoons did. We had to stop whatever the monsters were trying to do.

I had no idea if they had a conscious plan or were just driven by instincts. I tapped my nails on the bench. But I'd find out. I'd find out everything.

And Hunter Squad would stop them.

"Jess?" One of the technicians turned a comp screen my way. "These are the latest test results."

I looked at the screen and studied the data. I frowned at her. "The animal is in some sort of stasis."

The tech nodded. "Almost like a coma. Its vitals are stable, but slow. Slow heart rate, slow respiration."

This cocoon was definitely designed to keep whatever was inside it alive.

"Send these results through to Maxim as well. He was going to take a look at them." I was hoping the engineer and his genius IQ could help shed some light on this.

There was the rap of knuckles and I glanced up. North stood in the lab doorway.

My belly swooped. He wore jeans, and a light-gray T-shirt. Both molded to his muscular form. My gaze snagged on the tattoo on his arm. God, he looked good.

And he was all mine.

"You're a lucky woman," the tech murmured.

North walked toward me. I met him halfway and gave him a quick kiss. "Hey."

"Hi. I'm here to report that our request to move into one house was approved."

"That's great."

"I spoke to Jameson, and he and the guys will help us move the rest of your stuff out of your place tomorrow."

Tomorrow was our day off. Excitement flitted through me. North's place was similar to mine and decorated in what I called "man style" aka simple and sparse. He'd told me to change or add whatever touches I wanted.

He wanted to make it ours. Make it our home.

"And I'm also here because we've been summoned to a meeting with the generals," he added.

I nodded and slipped off my lab coat. When I turned, North was studying the cocoon.

"There's really a kangaroo in there?"

"There is. And it's very much alive."

He pulled a face. "Doesn't seem right to leave it in there."

"I know, but studying it could save human lives. We have to know what these cocoons do."

We headed out of the lab and down the corridor toward the command room.

"Colbie's been blowing up my communicator," I told him. "I've been invited to girls' night at Hemi's tonight. From what I can tell, there will be lots of cocktails involved, and I can't say no."

He smiled. "I'm meeting Zeke for a workout later. So, I'll be waiting for you when you get home."

Home. I really liked the sound of that.

He leaned in close. "Promise to be a little tipsy? I'll let you take advantage of me."

I laughed. "We'll see."

When the doors to the command room opened, I saw the rest of the squad was there, including Sasha, Colbie, and Maxim. Marcus and Cruz were also standing nearby with their arms crossed. My uncle gave me a chin lift.

"All right, everyone," General Masters said. "We've read Jameson's report on the rescue near Picton last night. Good work."

"North, are you okay?" General Stillman asked, concern on her face.

He nodded. "Thankfully, I wasn't in the cocoon for more than a few minutes before the guys got me out."

General Masters leveled his serious gaze on me. "And you have a cocoon in the lab?"

"Yes. It contains a live kangaroo. All the animal's

vitals have slowed down. Its heart rate, respiration, digestion, everything is low. It's alive, but in some sort of stasis or coma state."

General Masters' brows drew together and he shared a glance with his wife. "Why?"

I shook my head. "That, I can't answer. Not yet."

"We are extremely worried about these cocoons and the missing people." General Stillman frowned. "And the fact that the monsters you fought at the orchard appeared to be able to mask their heat signatures."

Sasha nodded. "They seemed to be in hiding, and appeared out of nowhere. It puts us at a big disadvantage. We've always relied on heat signatures to track them."

"Sounds like we need a new way to detect them," Maxim murmured. I could see the inventor was already considering possible solutions.

"You think you can come up with something?" General Masters asked.

Maxim shrugged. "I'll see."

Zeke stepped forward and everyone looked his way. The quiet man didn't say much, so I figured this was important. "At the orchard, Jess and I saw a monster. It didn't engage in the fight."

"God, yes." I'd almost forgotten about it with everything that had happened. "It was watching us, and it felt...intelligent."

Zeke nodded.

"Can you give us a description?" General Stillman asked.

I shook my head. "No, it stayed in the darkness. It

didn't come out of the shadows and it didn't fight. It was watching."

Zeke crossed his brawny arms. "It was tall, humanoid, and looked like it had wings. That's all I could tell."

General Stillman pressed her hands to the table. "Was it one of the monsters that created the cocoons?"

I shook my head. "No, I don't think so."

"I'd like to get my hands on those ugly fuckers," North muttered.

"We're calling them threaders," General Stillman said.

"Catchy," Jameson grunted.

"The monster with wings," Marcus asked in his gravelly voice. "Could it have been scared off by the fighting?"

"It wasn't scared," I said. "Sorry, that was just a feeling I got. I don't have any evidence."

"Gut feeling has saved our lives more than once," Uncle Cruz said.

"Okay, I want everyone to keep an eye out for this winged monster and the threaders," General Masters said. "Our priority is stopping them snatching people and putting them in cocoons."

"We think it's best that you capture a threader," General Stillman continued. "Alive."

I straightened and looked at my squad mates.

"Alive?" Marc pulled a face. "Great."

Jameson nodded. "We'll make a plan to do that."

"We'll have to find one first," North said.

"Oh, we'll find one," Jameson said. "Humanity

survived the Gizzida, and have built a new life, and now it's up to us to do our bit to protect it."

General Masters nodded. "I never doubted for a second that Hunter Squad wouldn't be able to handle this. Now, I believe you're all off the clock. Go. Enjoy your well-earned days off."

Marcus and Cruz stayed to talk with the generals. The rest of us headed out into the corridor.

"I think we all need to blow off some steam," Marc said. "And celebrate North and Jess losing their minds and shacking up together."

North shot his friend the finger.

"You don't need much of an excuse for a party," I noted.

Marc winked and slung an arm across my shoulders. "Life's too short, Ms. Ramos." He glanced at the others. "Everyone's invited to a barbecue at my place this evening."

"Wait," Colbie said. "We already have a girls' night at Hemi's planned. Me, Sash, and Jess."

"So, have your drinks and come for dinner afterward, lark," Marc said. "We'll have steak, chicken, prawns."

"Prawns? Those ones you marinate in butter and garlic?" The pilot looked torn.

"Those are the ones."

Colbie huffed. "Fine, I'll be there, after cocktails."

"Maybe I'm thirsty too," Marc said. "I like cocktails."

Colbie wagged a finger. "Girls only. You definitely don't have the right equipment."

I leaned into North, smiling as I listened to Colbie and Marc bickering. I felt a sense of belonging. I belonged right here. With my new friends, and a man I was already on the way to falling in love with.

I knew that my mom and dad would be happy.

"Ready to head home?" I asked.

He smiled. "With you, always."

The monsters couldn't destroy us. They'd never understand friendship and loyalty. Never understand how much we had to fight for.

And they'd definitely never understand love.

CHAPTER SIXTEEN

North

When I stepped into Hemi's, the smell of beer and the sound of laughter hit me.

It was busy as usual and filled with the after-work crowd. I'd finished my workout in the gym with Zeke and showered. Jess had left me a note to say she'd gone to girls' night, and that she'd see me at Marc's barbecue.

I grinned. It was nice to come home and see her makeup in the bathroom, some of her clothes in the closet, and a note that told me she was thinking of me.

I couldn't wait until the barbecue to see her. There was nothing that said a man couldn't pop into a bar for one quick drink.

Scanning the place, I spotted her by the bar. My body clenched. She was wearing a tiny pink dress, and the fabric shimmered under the lights. Tiny straps showed off toned shoulders, and her dark hair spilled down her back.

My chest locked. This was the woman that I'd love for the rest of my life.

Nothing had ever felt this right. I took a step forward.

"Hold it, buster." A short redhead slapped a hand to my chest. It took me a second to realize it was Colbie. She looked different with her sunset-red hair loose and wearing a green dress. It had a neckline that tied up behind her neck.

She aimed a scowl my way.

"Which part of girls' night didn't you understand?" she asked tartly.

"I'm not going to ruin your night. I'm just here, separately, to get a drink."

A snort came from the table beside us and I glanced at Sasha. She looked lovely in a red sequined top that contrasted with her black curls.

"The barbecue is in an hour," Colbie said.

I looked back at Jess. "I couldn't wait that long."

Colbie sighed. "You're a goner."

"Yep." I'd happily tell anybody who'd listened that I was gone for Jess Ramos.

Our pilot's lips twitched. "I'm happy that you found someone, North. I like seeing you in love."

I smiled and bopped her on the nose. "Me too."

She shook her head. "It's lucky you're handsome and I like looking at you." She stepped back and joined Sasha at the table. "Go get your girl."

That's when I saw the cocky firefighter from the other night step up to join Jess at the bar. He pressed a hand to her shoulder.

My smile snapped into a frown. *Hell, no.* I strode

across the bar, pressed in close to Jess, and slid my arm around her waist. "There you are."

Her eyes widened and she smiled up at me. "Hi."

I shot Mr. Casanova a hard look, then pressed my mouth to hers. I kissed her, pulling in the taste of her.

When I lifted my head, she was breathless. "He's gone."

"Good, but the kiss was for me, not him."

I curved my hand around her hip, then slid my fingers down to the short hem of her dress. I fiddled with it, then stroked her thigh. "I really like your dress."

Her lips parted. "I'm glad."

I stroked her again. "Your skin is so smooth." I inched upward.

She grabbed my wrist. "What are you doing here. I thought we'd agreed to meet at Marc's."

"I missed you."

With a soft look, she pressed into my arms. "I might've missed you too, but I was having a good time with Sasha and Colbie."

"I'm not surprised. They're fun."

She dragged in a deep breath, pressing her face against my neck. "You smell good." She tilted her head. "I kind of like it that you came to find me. Don't tell Colbie."

"I won't." I nibbled her lips. She tasted like coconut and rum.

"I really, really like you, North Connors."

I slid my hand along her jaw. "Think you could love me?"

"Yes. I think I'm partway there already."

"Good." I kissed her again.

"You're mine now, North. Don't forget it." She slid her arm through mine. "How about we get the girls and head to the barbecue?"

Marc

I FLIPPED THE STEAKS, flames rising on the grill.

Mmm. It smelled good. I was damn talented at cooking steak.

Around me, my friends were all having a good time. I kept my small backyard mowed and tidy. I didn't have time for garden beds, flowers, and that kind of shit, but I was pretty proud of my healthy, green grass.

I glanced around and instantly my gaze snagged on North and Jess. The couple was nuzzling each other. They looked ridiculously happy. I shook my head. There were so many lovely ladies around, so I didn't understand picking just one. Still, I was happy they were happy.

Beside me, Zeke made a grumpy sound. He was manning the second grill and scowling at the prawns.

I sighed. He was moody tonight. I was used to it. Sometimes, my brother could get lost in his head. I could usually poke at him and joke enough to get him out of it.

He'd always been quiet, but I knew the exact moment it had gotten worse. We'd been twelve and at Kai's sister's birthday party. The birthday girl had wandered off picking wildflowers and Zeke had noticed. He'd followed her.

They'd been snatched by a monster and dragged into the forest. They'd survived the three-day ordeal, but it had marked Zeke. I remembered how scared I'd been, remembered my mom crying. My hand curled into a fist. I'd been sure that I was going to lose my twin.

But my dad and Hell Squad had gone out to find them.

Zeke glanced up, like he'd sensed something, and stared across the party. I turned to follow his gaze. Amaia was smiling, standing beside Kai. The beautiful woman wore a blue dress, her white-blonde hair up in a twist, as she chatted with Jameson and Greer.

Amaia and Zeke had survived, had kept each other alive. They had a special bond because of it. Of course, Amaia didn't seem to realize that my hard-headed brother was in love with her.

Hell, I didn't think Zeke realized he was in love with her. Or if he did, he wasn't admitting it. He didn't let people get too close. He didn't date, he didn't fuck.

And he sure as hell hadn't made a move on Amaia.

Me, I liked to have fun. I flipped the steaks. Life was dangerous and could be too damn short. My uncle Zeke, dad's twin, had been killed by the Gizzida. I knew it still hurt my dad and that he missed his brother to this day.

Living life to the fullest was my way to honor the uncle I'd never had the chance to meet. No one was promised tomorrow. I liked to wring everything I could from life. My motto was to have fun, enjoy the ladies, hang with my friends, eat good steak.

"Why don't you go and talk to her?" I said.

Zeke glared at me and didn't say a word.

I held up the tongs. "Fine. Forget I said anything. Watch the steaks, I'm going to get a drink."

Leaving Zeke in charge, I headed for the coolers. They were packed with ice and bottles of Hemi's beer. I grabbed one, opened it, and took a long sip.

"Now, there's a handsome man," a female voice drawled.

Smiling, I turned. "I could show you a good time, darlin'."

My mom smiled and shook her head. "You have too much charm and too much sass in you."

I hugged her tightly. She smelled like mom—flowers with an undertone of antiseptic. It was the scent of my childhood. "I get it from you."

"You sure do. You definitely don't get it from your father."

Beside her, my dad made a low sound.

Gabe Jackson was six-and-a-half feet tall and still packed with muscle. He was part African American, which had given Zeke and I our brown skin, although dad was several shades darker. He kept his head shaved, which made him look even more badass. Zeke and I had also inherited his height and his gray eyes.

"Hi, Dad." I threw an arm out and we slapped each other on the back.

"Need help with the grill?" he asked. "Your Mom made me carry in three tons of salad."

Mom rolled her eyes.

"You could check on Zeke," I said. "He's in a mood tonight."

Dad stroked mom's hair, and for such a small gesture,

there was so much love loaded in it. My dad always looked at Mom like she was something incredible and he couldn't quite believe she was in his life. He headed off to help Zeke.

My mom gazed across the party with a concerned look for her second son.

"You know how Zeke gets. He'll snap out of it."

She nodded. "I know. He's so much like his father. Stews on everything." She focused on me. "How are you?"

I smiled. "Living my best life." Then over her shoulder, I saw Colbie walk in. I blinked. She was wearing a small, green dress that hugged her slim form. It tied up with a bow behind her neck, which just itched to be pulled free. She looked...hot.

Then I spotted the man beside her. She was holding some douchebag's hand.

My gaze narrowed. I didn't know him, but he looked like a stiff wind would blow him over and wore a pair of heavy-framed glasses. His jeans had neat creases in them. I could almost see the word Geek glowing in bright letters above him.

"Marc?"

"Huh?" I blinked and realized that Mom was looking at me.

She studied me hard. "Are you all right?"

"Yes." I cleared my throat, keeping an eye on Colbie and the guy. "What would you like to drink?"

"I'm okay. I see Greer has a bottle of wine open. I'll get a glass from her."

"I'll check on the steaks. Dad always overcooks

them." But I didn't head for the grill. Instead, I headed toward Colbie. She and her date were chatting with Sasha and Maxim.

"Evening, lark."

She turned and rolled her eyes.

"You're going to sprain something if you keep that up," I warned her.

"Marc, this is Spencer. He's a drone technician."

"Hello." Spencer pushed his glasses up the bridge of his nose and nodded. "Nice barbecue."

I lifted my chin.

"Marc's a member of Hunter Squad," Colbie said.

I slapped the man on the back. "Welcome, Spence."

Maybe my slap was a little hard. Spencer stumbled forward.

Colbie's gaze narrowed on me. "Aren't you needed at the grill?"

"Nope."

She bristled. Every time she did that I felt a shot of anticipation. I waited to see what would come out of her mouth.

Instead, there was the ping of the communicator. Colbie gave me one hot glare, then pulled her comm unit out. Her face fell. "Crap."

"What's wrong?" I asked.

"I'm on standby tonight. A couple of the pilots are out with the flu."

For all our technology and nano-meds, we still hadn't managed to find a cure for the flu.

"I'm needed to make an emergency supply drop to a

small community in the Blue Mountains." She looked at Spencer. "I'm sorry, I have to go."

Spencer nodded. "I'll give you a ride."

I stepped closer. "They need you to fly tonight?"

She nodded. "It's a shipment of urgent medicines. Save me some prawns."

She waved her goodbyes, and I watched her leave with her geek in tow.

"Who's the guy?" I muttered.

"He works on the drones," Sasha said. "He's kinda cute. They've been out for coffee a couple of times."

I grunted.

"Steaks are ready," Zeke called out.

Soon, everyone was sitting at the long table I'd set up in the yard. There were heavily-loaded plates of meat and bowls of salad courtesy of my parents. Everyone was laughing and having a fun time.

This. This was why I picked up a carbine. To protect this. The small moments that mattered.

That's when I heard a communicator ping. Then another. Mine vibrated in my pocket.

I groaned. "We're supposed to be done for the night."

"Monsters don't take time off," Jameson said.

Everyone on Hunter Squad pulled out their comm units, but Jameson was already reading his. He stood, and the grim look on his face made me tense.

"Hunter Squad, we need to go," he said.

I rose. "What's wrong?"

His gaze met mine. "Colbie's Talon went down."

My ears filled with static. "What?"

"She made a mayday call en route to the supply drop.

Her Talon crashed and we've lost communication with her."

"Oh, no," my mom said. My dad wrapped an arm around her.

I couldn't breathe. *Colbie. Crashed.* "Who was with her?"

"No one." A muscle ticked in Jameson's jaw. "She was alone. She crashed in the middle of the Blue Mountains."

My chest burned. She'd crashed in an area infested with monsters.

I pushed back from the table. "Let's go and bring her home."

"We'll clean up here," Mom said. "Go."

With a nod, I strode toward the house. Resolve filled me.

I was going to bring my lark home.

I hope you enjoyed Jess and North's story!

Hunter Squad continues with **MARC**, coming in late 2025/early 2026. Stay tuned for more monster-hunting action.

If you'd like to know more about the alien invasion, Marcus Steele, and Hell Squad, then check out the first Hell Squad book, *Marcus*. **Read on for a preview of the first chapter.**

Don't miss out! For updates about new releases, free books, and other fun stuff, sign up for my VIP mailing list and get your *free box set* containing three action-packed romances.

Visit here to get started: www.annahackett.com

Would you like a FREE BOX SET of my books?

PREVIEW: MARCUS

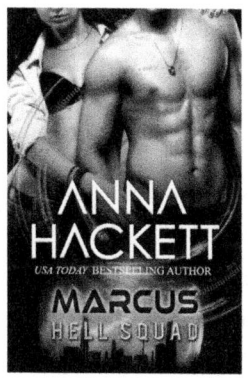

Her team was under attack.

Elle Milton pressed her fingers to her small earpiece. "Squad Six, you have seven more raptors inbound from the east." Her other hand gripped the edge of her comp screen, showing the enhanced drone feed.

She watched, her belly tight, as seven glowing red dots converged on the blue ones huddled together in the burned-out ruin of an office building in downtown

Sydney. Each blue dot was a squad member and one of them was their leader.

"Marcus? Do you copy?" Elle fought to keep her voice calm. No way she'd let them hear her alarm.

"Roger that, Elle." Marcus' gravelly voice filled her ear. Along with the roar of laser fire. "We see them."

She sagged back in her chair. This was the worst part. Just sitting there knowing that Marcus and the others were fighting for their lives. In the six months she'd been comms officer for the squad, she'd worked hard to learn the ropes. But there were days she wished she was out there, aiming a gun and taking out as many alien raptors as she could.

You're not a soldier, Ellianna. No, she was a useless party-girl-turned-survivor. She watched as a red dot disappeared off the screen, then another, and another. She finally drew a breath. Marcus and his team were the experienced soldiers. She'd just be a big fat liability in the field.

But she was a damn good comms officer.

Just then, a new cluster of red dots appeared near the team. She tapped the screen, took a measurement. "Marcus! More raptors are en route. They're about one kilometer away. North." God, would these invading aliens ever leave them alone?

"Shit," Marcus bit out. Then he went silent.

She didn't know if he was thinking or fighting. She pictured his rugged, scarred face creased in thought as he formulated a plan.

Then his deep, rasping voice was back. "Elle, we need an escape route and an evac now. Shaw's been hit in the leg, Cruz is carrying him. We can't engage more raptors."

She tapped the screen rapidly, pulling up drone images and archived maps. *Escape route, escape route.* Her mind clicked through the options. She knew Shaw was taller and heavier than Cruz, but the armor they wore had slim-line exoskeletons built into them allowing the soldiers to lift heavier loads and run faster and longer than normal. She tapped the screen again. *Come on.* She needed somewhere safe for a Hawk quadcopter to set down and pick them up.

"Elle? We need it now!"

Just then her comp beeped. She looked at the image and saw a hazy patch of red appear in the broken shell of a nearby building. The heat sensor had detected something else down there. Something big.

Right next to the team.

She touched her ear. "Rex! Marcus, a rex has just woken up in the building beside you."

"Fuck! Get us out of here. Now."

Oh, God. Elle swallowed back bile. Images of rexes, with their huge, dinosaur-like bodies and mouths full of teeth, flashed in her head.

More laser fire ripped through her earpiece and she heard the wild roar of the awakening beast.

Block it out. She focused on the screen. Marcus needed her. The team needed her.

"Run past the rex." One hand curled into a tight fist, her nails cutting into her skin. "Go through its hiding place."

PREVIEW: MARCUS

"Through its nest?" Marcus' voice was incredulous. "You know how territorial they are."

"It's the best way out. On the other side you'll find a railway tunnel. Head south along it about eight hundred meters, and you'll find an emergency exit ladder that you can take to the surface. I'll have a Hawk pick you up there."

A harsh expulsion of breath. "Okay, Elle. You've gotten us out of too many tight spots for me to doubt you now."

His words had heat creeping into her cheeks. His praise...it left her giddy. In her life BAI—before alien invasion—no one had valued her opinions. Her father, her mother, even her almost-fiancé, they'd all thought her nothing more than a pretty ornament. Hell, she *had* been a silly, pretty party girl.

And because she'd been inept, her parents were dead. Elle swallowed. A year had passed since that horrible night during the first wave of the alien attack, when their giant ships had appeared in the skies. Her parents had died that night, along with most of the world.

"Hell Squad, ready to go to hell?" Marcus called out.

"Hell, yeah!" the team responded. "The devil needs an ass-kicking!"

"Woo-hoo!" Another voice blasted through her headset, pulling her from the past. "Ellie, baby, this dirty alien's nest stinks like Cruz's socks. You should be here."

A smile tugged at Elle's lips. Shaw Baird always knew how to ease the tension of a life-or-death situation.

"Oh, yeah, Hell Squad gets the best missions," Shaw added.

PREVIEW: MARCUS

Elle watched the screen, her smile slipping. Everyone called Squad Six the Hell Squad. She was never quite sure if it was because they were hellions, or because they got sent into hell to do the toughest, dirtiest missions.

There was no doubt they were a bunch of rebels. Marcus had a rep for not following orders. Just the previous week, he'd led the squad in to destroy a raptor outpost but had detoured to rescue survivors huddled in an abandoned hospital that was under attack. At the debrief, the general's yelling had echoed through the entire base. Marcus, as always, had been silent.

"Shut up, Shaw, you moron." The deep female voice carried an edge.

Elle had decided there were two words that best described the only female soldier on Hell Squad—loner and tough. Claudia Frost was everything Elle wasn't. Elle cleared her throat. "Just get yourselves back to base."

As she listened to the team fight their way through the rex nest, she tapped in the command for one of the Hawk quadcopters to pick them up.

The line crackled. "Okay, Elle, we're through. Heading to the evac point."

Marcus' deep voice flowed over her and the tense muscles in her shoulders relaxed a fraction. They'd be back soon. They were okay. He was okay.

She pressed a finger to the blue dot leading the team. "The bird's en route, Marcus."

"Thanks. See you soon."

She watched on the screen as the large, black shadow of the Hawk hovered above the ground and the team

PREVIEW: MARCUS

boarded. The rex was headed in their direction, but they were already in the air.

Elle stood and ran her hands down her trousers. She shot a wry smile at the camouflage fabric. It felt like a dream to think that she'd ever owned a very expensive, designer wardrobe. And heels—God, how long had it been since she'd worn heels? These days, fatigues were all that hung in her closet. Well-worn ones, at that.

As she headed through the tunnels of the underground base toward the landing pads, she forced herself not to run. She'd see him—them—soon enough. She rounded a corner and almost collided with someone.

"General. Sorry, I wasn't watching where I was going."

"No problem, Elle." General Adam Holmes had a military-straight bearing he'd developed in the United Coalition Army and a head of dark hair with a brush of distinguished gray at his temples. He was classically handsome, and his eyes were a piercing blue. He was the top man in this last little outpost of humanity. "Squad Six on their way back?"

"Yes, sir." They fell into step.

"And they secured the map?"

God, Elle had almost forgotten about the map. "Ah, yes. They got images of it just before they came under attack by raptors."

"Well, let's go welcome them home. That map might just be the key to the fate of mankind."

They stepped into the landing areas. Staff in various military uniforms and civilian clothes raced around. After the raptors had attacked, bringing all manner of

PREVIEW: MARCUS

vicious creatures with them to take over the Earth, what was left of mankind had banded together.

Whoever had survived now lived here in an underground base in the Blue Mountains, just west of Sydney, or in the other, similar outposts scattered across the planet. All arms of the United Coalition's military had been decimated. In the early days, many of the surviving soldiers had fought amongst themselves, trying to work out who outranked whom. But it didn't take long before General Holmes had unified everyone against the aliens. Most squads were a mix of ranks and experience, but the teams eventually worked themselves out. Most didn't even bother with titles and rank anymore.

Sirens blared, followed by the clang of metal. Huge doors overhead retracted into the roof.

A Hawk filled the opening, with its sleek gray body and four spinning rotors. It was near-silent, running on a small thermonuclear engine. It turned slowly as it descended to the landing pad.

Her team was home.

She threaded her hands together, her heart beating a little faster.

Marcus was home.

Marcus Steele wanted a shower and a beer.

Hot, sweaty and covered in raptor blood, he leaped down from the Hawk and waved at his team to follow. He kept a sharp eye on the medical team who raced out to tend to Shaw. Dr. Emerson Green was leading them, her white lab coat snapping around her curvy body. The blonde doctor caught his gaze and tossed him a salute.

Shaw was cursing and waving them off, but one look from Marcus and the lanky Australian sniper shut his mouth.

Marcus swung his laser carbine over his shoulder and scraped a hand down his face. Man, he'd kill for a hot shower. Of course, he'd have to settle for a cold one since they only allowed hot water for two hours in the morning in order to conserve energy. But maybe after that beer he'd feel human again.

"Well done, Squad Six." Holmes stepped forward. "Steele, I hear you got images of the map."

Holmes might piss Marcus off sometimes, but at least the guy always got straight to the point. He was a general to the bone and always looked spit and polish. Everything about him screamed money and a fancy education, so not surprisingly, he tended to rub the troops the wrong way.

Marcus pulled the small, clear comp chip from his pocket. "We got it."

Then he spotted her.

Shit. It was always a small kick in his chest. His gaze traveled up Elle Milton's slim figure, coming to rest on a face he could stare at all day. She wasn't very tall, but that didn't matter. Something about her high cheekbones, pale-blue eyes, full lips, and rain of chocolate-brown hair…it all worked for him. Perfectly. She was beautiful, kind, and far too good to be stuck in this crappy underground maze of tunnels, dressed in hand-me-down fatigues.

She raised a slim hand. Marcus shot her a small nod.

"Hey, Ellie-girl. Gonna give me a kiss?"

Shaw passed on an iono-stretcher hovering off the ground and Marcus gritted his teeth. The tall, blond sniper with his lazy charm and Aussie drawl was popular with the ladies. Shaw flashed his killer smile at Elle.

She smiled back, her blue eyes twinkling and Marcus' gut cramped.

Then she put one hand on her hip and gave the sniper a head-to-toe look. She shook her head. "I think you get enough kisses."

Marcus released the breath he didn't realize he was holding.

"See you later, Sarge." Zeke Jackson slapped Marcus on the back and strolled past. His usually-silent twin, Gabe, was beside him. The twins, both former Coalition Army Special Forces soldiers, were deadly in the field. Marcus was damned happy to have them on his squad.

"Howdy, Princess." Claudia shot Elle a smirk as she passed.

Elle rolled her eyes. "Claudia."

Cruz, Marcus' second-in-command and best friend from their days as Coalition Marines, stepped up beside Marcus and crossed his arms over his chest. He'd already pulled some of his lightweight body armor off, and the ink on his arms was on display.

The general nodded at Cruz before looking back at Marcus. "We need Shaw back up and running ASAP. If the raptor prisoner we interrogated is correct, that map shows one of the main raptor communications hubs." There was a blaze of excitement in the usually-stoic general's voice. "It links all their operations together."

Yeah, Marcus knew it was big. Destroy the hub, send the raptor operations into disarray.

The general continued. "As soon as the tech team can break the encryption on the chip and give us a location for the raptor comms hub—" his piercing gaze leveled on Marcus "—I want your team back out there to plant the bomb."

Marcus nodded. He knew if they destroyed the raptors' communications it gave humanity a fighting chance. A chance they desperately needed.

He traded a look with Cruz. Looked like they were going out to wade through raptor gore again sooner than anticipated.

Man, he really wanted that beer.

Then Marcus' gaze landed on Elle again. He didn't keep going out there for himself, or Holmes. He went so people like Elle and the other civilian survivors had a chance. A chance to do more than simply survive.

"Shaw's wound is minor. Doc Emerson should have him good as new in an hour or so." Since the advent of the nano-meds, simple wounds could be healed in hours, rather than days and weeks. They carried a dose of the microscopic medical machines on every mission, but only for dire emergencies. The nano-meds had to be administered and monitored by professionals or they were just as likely to kill you from the inside than heal you.

General Holmes nodded. "Good."

Elle cleared her throat. "There's no telling how long it will take to break the encryption. I've been working with the tech team and even if they break it, we may not be able to translate it all. We're getting better at learning the raptor language but there are still huge amounts of it we don't yet understand."

Marcus' jaw tightened. There was always something. He knew Noah Kim—their resident genius computer specialist—and his geeks were good, but if they couldn't read the damn raptor language...

Holmes turned. "Steele, let your team have some downtime and be ready the minute Noah has anything."

"Yes, sir." As the general left, Marcus turned to Cruz. "Go get yourself a beer, Ramos."

"Don't need to tell me more than once, *amigo*. I would kill for some of my dad's tamales to go with it." Something sad flashed across a face all the women in the base mooned over, then he grimaced and a bone-deep weariness colored his words. "Need to wash the raptor off me, first." He tossed Marcus a casual salute, Elle a smile, and strode out.

Marcus frowned after his friend and absently started loosening his body armor.

Elle moved up beside him. "I can take the comp chip to Noah."

"Sure." He handed it to her. When her fingers brushed his he felt the warmth all the way through him. Hell, he had it bad. Thankfully, he still had his armor on or she'd see his cock tenting his pants.

"I'll come find you as soon as we have something." She glanced up at him. Smiled. "Are you going to rec night tonight? I hear Cruz might even play guitar for us."

The Friday-night gathering was a chance for everyone to blow off a bit of steam and drink too much homebrewed beer. And Cruz had an unreal talent with a guitar, although lately Marcus hadn't seen the man play too much.

Marcus usually made an appearance at these parties, then left early to head back to his room to study raptor movements or plan the squad's next missions. "Yeah, I'll be there."

"Great." She smiled. "I'll see you there, then." She hurried out clutching the chip.

He stared at the tunnel where she'd exited for a long while after she disappeared, and finally ripped his chest armor off. Ah, on second thought, maybe going to the rec night wasn't a great idea. Watching her pretty face and captivating smile would drive him crazy. He cursed under his breath. He really needed that cold shower.

As he left the landing pads, he reminded himself he should be thinking of the mission. Destroy the hub and kill more aliens. Rinse and repeat. Death and killing, that was about all he knew.

He breathed in and caught a faint trace of Elle's floral scent. She was clean and fresh and good. She always worried about them, always had a smile, and she was damned good at providing their comms and intel.

She was why he fought through the muck every day. So she could live and the goodness in her would survive. She deserved more than blood and death and killing.

And she sure as hell deserved more than a battled-scarred, bloodstained soldier.

Hell Squad
Marcus

Cruz

PREVIEW: MARCUS

Gabe
Reed
Roth
Noah
Shaw
Holmes
Niko
Finn
Devlin
Theron
Hemi
Ash
Levi
Manu
Griff
Dom
Survivors
Tane
Also Available as Audiobooks!

ALSO BY ANNA HACKETT

Hunter Squad
Jameson

Fury Brothers
Fury

Keep

Burn

Take

Claim

Also Available as Audiobooks!

Unbroken Heroes
The Hero She Needs

The Hero She Wants

The Hero She Craves

The Hero She Deserves

The Hero She Loves

Also Available as Audiobooks!

Sentinel Security
Wolf

Hades

Striker

Steel

Excalibur

Hex

Stone

Also Available as Audiobooks!

Norcross Security

The Investigator

The Troubleshooter

The Specialist

The Bodyguard

The Hacker

The Powerbroker

The Detective

The Medic

The Protector

Mr. & Mrs. Norcross

Also Available as Audiobooks!

Billionaire Heists

Stealing from Mr. Rich

Blackmailing Mr. Bossman

Hacking Mr. CEO

Also Available as Audiobooks!

Team 52

Mission: Her Protection

Mission: Her Rescue

Mission: Her Security

Mission: Her Defense

Mission: Her Safety

Mission: Her Freedom

Mission: Her Shield

Mission: Her Justice

Also Available as Audiobooks!

Treasure Hunter Security

Undiscovered

Uncharted

Unexplored

Unfathomed

Untraveled

Unmapped

Unidentified

Undetected

Also Available as Audiobooks!

Oronis Knights

Knightmaster

Knighthunter

Galactic Kings

Overlord

Emperor

Captain of the Guard

Conqueror

Also Available as Audiobooks!

Eon Warriors

Edge of Eon

Touch of Eon

Heart of Eon

Kiss of Eon

Mark of Eon

Claim of Eon

Storm of Eon

Soul of Eon

King of Eon

Also Available as Audiobooks!

Galactic Gladiators: House of Rone

Sentinel

Defender

Centurion

Paladin

Guard

Weapons Master

Also Available as Audiobooks!

Galactic Gladiators

Gladiator

Warrior

Hero

Protector

Champion

Barbarian

Beast

Rogue

Guardian

Cyborg

Imperator

Hunter

Also Available as Audiobooks!

Hell Squad

Marcus

Cruz

Gabe

Reed

Roth

Noah

Shaw

Holmes

Niko

Finn

Devlin

Theron

Hemi

Ash

Levi

Manu

Griff

Dom

Survivors

Tane

Also Available as Audiobooks!

The Anomaly Series

Time Thief

Mind Raider

Soul Stealer

Salvation

Anomaly Series Box Set

The Phoenix Adventures

Among Galactic Ruins

At Star's End

In the Devil's Nebula

On a Rogue Planet

Beneath a Trojan Moon

Beyond Galaxy's Edge
On a Cyborg Planet
Return to Dark Earth
On a Barbarian World
Lost in Barbarian Space
Through Uncharted Space
Crashed on an Ice World

Perma Series

Winter Fusion
A Galactic Holiday

Warriors of the Wind

Tempest
Storm & Seduction
Fury & Darkness

Standalone Titles

Savage Dragon
Hunter's Surrender
One Night with the Wolf

For more information visit www.annahackett.com

ABOUT THE AUTHOR

I'm a USA Today bestselling romance author who's passionate about ***fast-paced, emotion-filled*** contemporary romantic suspense and science fiction romance. I love writing about people overcoming unbeatable odds and achieving seemingly impossible goals. I like to believe it's possible for all of us to do the same.

I live in Australia with my own personal hero and two very busy, always-on-the-move sons.

For release dates, behind-the-scenes info, free books, and other fun stuff, sign up for the latest news here:

Website: www.annahackett.com

Printed in Great Britain
by Amazon